Praise for the Resurrec

SNAKE PASS:

"Crackerjack entertainment: taut, gritty and full of devilish twists."—*Kirkus Reviews*

ADOBE FLATS:

"A stylish noir voice."—*Kirkus Reviews*

MONTECITO HEIGHTS:

"Wry maverick Grant never fails to entertain."—*Kirkus Reviews*

"This gritty thriller ... maintains a breakneck pace ... [and] its smart structure and unrelenting suspense will please Lee Child fans."—*Library Journal*

JAMAICA PLAIN:

"Grim and gritty and packed with action and crackling dialogue."—*Kirkus Reviews*

"Campbell hits a high note with his gritty novel that catches the atmosphere of Jamaica Plain, Boston, and turns it into a compelling account of murder, sex and violence."—*RT Book Reviews*

"Very real. Very good."—*Lee Child, New York Times bestselling author of the Reacher Novels*

A RESURRECTION MAN NOVEL

COLIN CAMPBELL

MIDNIGHT INK
WOODBURY, MINNESOTA

FIRST EDITION
First Printing, 2015

Cover design: Kevin R. Brown
Cover illustration: Dominick Finelle/July Group

Midnight Ink, an imprint of Llewellyn Worldwide Ltd.

Library of Congress Cataloging-in-Publication Data
Campbell, Colin, 1955–
Snake pass : a resurrection man novel / Colin Campbell.—First edition.
pages ; cm.—(A resurrection man novel; #4)
Summary: "Yorkshire cop Jim Grant will do anything to bring down the bad guys. But when the Discipline and Complaint inspector feels he's gone too far, Grant is put on suspension and goes to his favorite all-night diner to flirt with his favorite waitress…and that's when all hell breaks loose"—Publisher.
ISBN 978-0-7387-4346-2
I. Title.
PR6103.A48S63 2015
823'.92—dc23

2014039180

Midnight Ink
Llewellyn Worldwide Ltd.
2143 Wooddale Drive
Woodbury, MN 55125-2989

www.midnightinkbooks.com

Printed in the United States of America

For Donna:
more than an agent;
not just a friend.
Thanks.

There's always a way of getting the job done. Nose to the grindstone trumps thumb up the arse every time.

—Jim Grant

21:50 HOURS

Jim Grant was pissed off long before he got to Snake Pass on Thursday night. Before the snow began to fall and the entire world decided to shoot it out at the Woodlands Truck Stop and Diner. He was already pissed off three hours earlier when he parked his patrol car across the mouth of Edgebank Close and turned the engine off. Ravenscliffe Avenue stretched out behind him like a nighttime runway with half the lights missing. Ravenscliffe woods bulked up against the night sky beyond the houses in the cul-de-sac. He was four hours into his ten-hour shift, a half-night tour of duty that started at six in the evening.

Being pissed off meant he wasn't going to make it until four.

PC Grant adjusted the stab vest under his uniform jacket and drummed the fingers of his right hand on the steering wheel. He stared at the house at the end of the short, stubby street. He looked calm and relaxed and completely un-pissed off on the outside. That was one of his strengths. It was why Sergeant Ballhaus had made him a tutor constable and why the fresh-faced young constable in the passenger seat didn't know to keep quiet.

"But isn't that unethical?"

"What?"

Constable Hope was carrying on the conversation they'd been having for most of the shift. Being eighteen years old and in the first six months of his service meant he didn't know when the subject was closed.

"Ignoring a crime just because you're off-duty?"

"I'm not saying you should ignore it. Just don't go charging in waving your warrant card with no radio and no backup."

"But your warrant card gives you authority as a police officer throughout England and Wales."

"Doesn't give you shit-all in a pub fight with no baton and stab vest."

"But—"

Grant held up a hand for Hope to be quiet.

"Case in point. Young copper I knew goes for Chinese down at Mean Wood junction. Pubs are shutting. Lot of drunks ordering takeaway. Trouble brews. A fight ensues. Young copper whips out his warrant card and orders them all to cease and desist. What do you think happened?"

Hope tried to keep the hero worship off his face. Listening to a legend of the West Yorkshire Police recounting tales of derring-do was like manna from heaven for the young probationer constable. He answered with a question.

"They didn't cease and desist?"

"They did not. He got the shit kicked out of him and spent three days in the hospital. The riot he provoked wrecked the Chinese place and two shops on either side of it and put everybody on double shifts for a week. Point is, drunks fighting each other are par for the course. Serves 'em right if they've got sore heads and a few bruises the following morning. It's no big deal."

"What about theft?"

"What about it?"

"Should you ignore a theft?"

Grant let out a sigh. This kid never gave up. It was one of the things Grant liked about him. He could be exasperating at times, though.

"Judgment call. Another example. Inspector Speedhoff was down at the supermarket with his kids, aged two and four. Spots some dickhead nicking citric acid for his drug habit. Wades in to make an off-duty arrest. What do you think happened?"

Hope smiled.

"He got the shit kicked out of him?"

"In front of his kids. They had nightmares for weeks. Citric acid isn't exactly the great train robbery. Let it slide. Or, if you feel strongly, tell the store detective. But don't go wading in without communication or backup. Off-duty is off-duty."

The engine purred. Exhaust fumes plumed into the cold Yorkshire air. The cul-de-sac was quiet. The house at the end of the street was mostly in darkness, apart from a light in the upstairs landing. Hope displayed why he was a prospect for the future and had been paired with Grant.

"Don't you think we should communicate for backup before we go in?"

"We're not off-duty."

Grant smiled at his protégé.

"And it's only an address check. We won't need backup."

Grant turned the engine off and looked at the house through the windscreen. Hot metal ticked and popped under the bonnet as the engine cooled. The veteran had been here many times before, but he examined the front of the house again anyway. Standard procedure before going into action, address check or not.

The house was a run-down three-bedroom semi, the left-hand half of the pair across the end of the cul-de-sac. The front aspect had a wide living room window and a narrow front door. Above them were the main bedroom window and the smaller spare room. Round the side of the house there was only a kitchen window and the upstairs landing window—the one with the light on. The kitchen door was in the rear aspect, hidden from view, but Grant knew what it looked like. Upstairs was the rear bedroom and the bathroom at the top of the stairs.

Lee Adkins could be hiding in any one of those rooms.

Grant stopped drumming his fingers and got out of the car. Hope got out of his side too. Both closed their doors quietly, making barely a click. The boy had smarts. Steam bloomed around his head in the cold night air as he waited for Grant's instructions. Standard deployment for a house search was one covering the back in case the suspect tried to escape. An address check was much more low-key. It didn't matter if someone jumped out of the back window. Except this wasn't really an address check.

"Go cover the back. You remember what I said?"

Hope nodded. "Stand at least six feet away from the house at the corner so I can see two aspects at the same time—the back and the side. But I thought this was just an address check?"

Grant pulled his black leather gloves on.

"Always best to be on the safe side."

"Everyone knows Lee Adkins lives here."

"Intelligence is only as good as the last time it was checked. You have to constantly update it. I'm updating it tonight. Now, get round the back."

Hope's shoulders sagged.

Grant was sorry he'd sounded so harsh. It was nothing personal. He just didn't want the young lad with him when he went in. Some things you don't need witnesses for. Some things you don't want to burden your probationer with. He watched Police Constable Jamie Hope walk down the side of the house and disappear into the gloom, then took the bloodstained bus pass out of his pocket. The shaved head and surly eyes of Lee Adkins stared out from the plastic wallet. The blood smeared across the plastic wasn't his.

THE SLAP ACROSS THE face knocked Sharon Davis off her feet in the foyer of the rugby club on Harrogate Road. The second slap wasn't a slap at all, it was a punch, and it was probably the blow that broke her nose and closed one eye. She kicked out in vain. Lee Adkins stepped in and thumped her three more times while she was on the floor. She stopped crying out after the second punch.

The club reception miraculously emptied. The few customers waiting to pass through into the lounge bar vanished. The old-age pensioner manning the signing-in book behind the counter went into the office. Nobody witnessed the assault. That's what the old man told Jim Grant when he responded to the report of a disturbance twenty minutes later.

Grant crouched beside the shivering mass of blood and flesh that had once been the prettiest teenager on the estate. Nineteen years old going on ninety. Grant comforted her as best he could until the ambulance arrived. She feigned memory loss, but Grant knew she wouldn't point the finger at the biggest thug in Ravenscliffe. The burgling, drug-dealing scumbucket Lee Adkins. Everyone was afraid of him. Everybody knew he was Sharon Davis's boyfriend.

After she'd been taken away, Grant let Hope take the report from the old man. A barebones affair that would be needed to write off the IBIS log back at the control room. There was enough evidence of an assault to record a crime, but with nobody willing to come forward as a witness and a complainant who was refusing to name her assailant, the statistics boys on the third floor would want to downgrade this from a Section 47 assault to a noisy disturbance. Meet the target figures for reducing violent crime.

Grant made enquiries in the office. The CCTV cameras that covered the club inside and out weren't recording tonight. There'd been plenty of recordings the night the club got burgled three weeks ago. That didn't surprise Grant. He'd been trying to nail Adkins for eighteen months, but you couldn't get a conviction without evidence or witnesses. Holding the estate in a grip of fear was the best protection the thieving bastard could have got. Except tonight he'd made a mistake.

The plastic wallet had been lying under Sharon Davis's crumpled body. Grant had picked it up when she was being carried to the ambulance. He flicked it open now while Hope finished taking the report. The cardboard bus pass was sealed inside the plastic. The shaved head and surly eyes stared up at him from the photograph. Lee Adkins's face was covered in blood, the fresh redness smeared across his image. Grant slipped the wallet into his pocket and smiled. He could sense a tactical address check coming on.

Grant closed the plastic wallet and put it back in his pocket. Hope was now safely out of the way. The house was still in darkness, apart from the light from the landing window. Grant flexed the fingers inside his leather gloves and took a deep breath. He let it out slowly, the cloud of vapor hiding his face for a moment, then strode down the garden path towards the front door.

He threw one last glance to make sure that Hope hadn't snuck down the side of the house. Some things you don't need witnesses for. It was an adage that Lee Adkins lived by. Grant was simply using the villain's strength against him. He raised his heavily booted foot and kicked the front door open.

22:00 HOURS

ADKINS WAS IN THE bathroom. Through the open door at the top of the stairs, Grant could see the bathroom light spilling out onto the landing. The front door smashed backwards against the side of the hallway, its frame splintered to oblivion. Shards of wood stood out like porcupine quills around the lock. The house was clean and tidy, in contrast to the drug addicts' homes that Adkins supplied. It smelled of soap and air freshener. Radio traffic squawked on Grant's shoulder, the rest of the shift going about its business, unaware of the drama unfolding at 5 Edgebank Close.

Grant flicked the hall and landing lights on and took the stairs two at a time. Speed was key once you'd forced the breach. Speed and light. He didn't want to be stumbling through the shadows with his target holding the high ground. He might have been here many times before, but you had to expect the unexpected. The roller skates on the stair bed or the tripwire across the risers. He reached the landing before the front door had stopped quivering.

Adkins stood up from the sink, his face dripping water.

Grant leaned on the bathroom doorframe.

"Cut yourself shaving?"

The water swirling down the plughole was pink. Splatters of red dotted the washbasin. Adkins held a white towel in one hand, the knuckles stained with Sharon Davis's blood, the towel painted in the stuff. Grant leaned forward, turned the tap off, and put the plug in. He snatched the towel out of Adkins's hand.

"You missed a bit."

He indicated the blood splatters on the side of Adkins face. He'd beaten the girl with such ferocity that the blowback had spread way beyond the knuckles that caused the damage. Blood that would tie him to the assault and prove the case if Sharon Davis hadn't been too frightened to bring a case against the burgling drug dealer. Grant made a snap decision. The blood on the towel and Adkins's knuckles would be enough.

He whipped his free hand up and grabbed Adkins behind the head. The leather glove snatched a handful of hair and slammed the burglar's face down into the sink. His nose and lip exploded. One eye swelled shut immediately.

"How do you like it, fuckface?"

Adkins was about to reply but Grant smashed his face into the sink again.

"That was a rhetorical question."

Adkins' knees buckled, and he flopped to the fluffy beige carpet that was now speckled with fresh blood. Grant was thinking clearly. He saw the drug dealer kneeling on the floor and the stripped pine bath panel in the background. He'd tried to get a search warrant for this house a dozen times but couldn't get the paperwork past the magistrate. There had never been enough evidence to prove that Adkins was involved with all the crimes he was involved in. The spoils of those crimes were hidden in this house. The drugs and the money.

Grant back-heeled the bath panel.

"Oops."

The top of the panel opened slightly, leaving a two-inch gap. The preferred hiding place for drug dealers ever since the toilet cistern had been exposed on too many TV shows. Grant heard footsteps charge through the front door and made another snap decision. He didn't want Hope getting caught having to lie about Adkins's injuries. He pressed the transmit button on his shoulder.

"Stop resisting."

Adkins threw Grant a confused look from the bathroom floor.

Grant kept his finger on the transmit button and spoke into the open mike.

"Put the weapon down. Don't—"

He turned his face to one side and head-butted the wall. The porcelain tiles cracked and cut his forehead. Releasing the transmit button, he reached down and grabbed Adkins's right arm, twisting it behind the fallen burglar's back. The footsteps bounded up the stairs. Grant could hear Hope shouting into his radio.

"Officers need assistance—5 Edgebank Close."

He didn't need to say urgent. Jane Archer knew that an officer-needs-assistance call was always urgent. The radio controller relayed the request over the airwaves, and every copper in Bradford stopped what they were doing and headed towards Ravenscliffe. That's the way it worked on the frontline. Grant felt a pang of guilt at setting that in motion, but he was already looking at the bigger picture.

Jamie Hope burst into the bathroom.

Grant held up one hand to calm the probationer's approach. He got to his feet, dragging Lee Adkins with him. He caught sight of his reflection in the wall mirror. Blood trickled down the side of his face from an ugly swelling above the right eye.

Hope's mouth dropped open.

"Are you all right?"

The most ridiculous question but also the most obvious. Grant decided to cut Hope some slack and not fire a sarcastic reply. He simply blinked his eyes instead of nodding, then jerked his head towards Adkins.

"You should see the other fella."

Hope regained his composure. "I can see the other fella. What happened?"

"Resisted arrest."

Hope showed again why he was a prospect for the future. He moved so that Grant blocked Adkins's view and lowered his voice.

"Arrest for what?"

Grant pointed at the gap in the bath panel and pulled it open another couple of inches, careful not to disturb any fingerprints that would prove Adkins had opened the panel before. The rolls of banknotes were barely visible through the gap, but the bags of white powder stood out even in the dim bathroom light.

"Eureka."

Hope proved he had a sense of humor to match his smarts.

"Wasn't that to do with water displacement in the bath? Not hidden drugs underneath it?"

Grant wiped the blood from his eye.

"Calculating weight by measuring displaced water—something like that. I'll bet there's enough weight in there to send this little bastard back to Her Majesty's school of hard knocks."

Adkins moaned. Hope kept his voice low.

"A bit careless of him, leaving it open like that."

Grant shrugged.

"Probably got dislodged during the struggle."

Grant could see where Hope was going with this and headed him off at the pass. He didn't want the young constable giving Adkins ideas for his defense. He held the bloodstained bus pass up.

"This is what got him arrested. The rest is just good luck."

Hope nodded that he understood. Another tick for Grant's tutor report. He put the plastic wallet back in his pocket.

"I'll bet a pound to a pinch of shit whose blood it is."

"Sharon Davis."

"You win. Now let's cuff this twat and cancel backup. We only need transport and an ambulance. Just make sure it's not the one that took her. We don't want to be accused of cross-contaminating blood samples."

Hope went outside to make the calls. The blood was a moot point since Grant had comforted the bleeding Davis at the crime scene. She wouldn't make the complaint anyway. It was the drugs that would send him to prison. Grant handcuffed Adkins's hands behind his back as blue lights began to flash in the street.

22:30 HOURS

"You know as well as I do that calling it forced entry to preserve evidence isn't gonna fly."

Sergeant Ballhaus stepped back from the landing to let the SOCO get to work with the blood samples trapped in the U-bend. The scenes-of-crime officer was careful where he knelt as he unscrewed the waste pipe. He wasn't dressed in the full forensic paper suit—this wasn't a murder scene—but he didn't want to get blood on his trousers.

Grant had bagged the bus pass for DNA testing himself to at least preserve the illusion of avoiding cross-contamination. Having the samples from the waste pipe and the bloody towel booked in by the same officer who had seized the bus pass at the crime scene would make it too easy for the defense solicitor to pick holes. There were enough holes already.

Grant stood in the doorway to the front bedroom.

"Worked, though, didn't it?"

He pointed towards the bathroom.

"The evidence is preserved."

Then he nodded at the bath panel, still open a few inches at the top.

"And I'm telling you, we're gonna hit the evidence jackpot."

Ballhaus let out an exasperated sigh and glanced over his shoulder to make sure that Jamie Hope had gone downstairs. He jerked a thumb towards the bedroom.

"Fuck me, Jim. Ways and Means Act doesn't work anymore."

Grant followed his sergeant into the front bedroom. He knew he was skating on thin ice but was confident that Ballhaus was a practical copper and not the pencil-pushing desk jockey that most supervisors became once they were off the frontline. A shift sergeant at Ecclesfield Division was about as frontline as it got.

"Sarge. There's always a way of getting the job done. Nose to the grindstone trumps thumb up the arse every time."

Ballhaus stood by the bedroom window and looked down at the sea of blue flashing lights. The paramedics had taken Adkins away but there were still three patrol cars and the divisional van choking the cul-de-sac. It was a testament to the code of the streets. When you called for backup, everyone responded. Ballhaus appeared to fill with pride that his boys honored that code. He turned back to face Grant.

"Jim. Grow up. This is the modern police force. There are more thumb-up-the-arse types than there are practical policing types. So let's not give them anything to poke shit-fingers at."

Grant nodded his understanding.

"Okay. Let's shape this right."

He rubbed his chin for a moment before clarifying the first point.

"Entry to preserve evidence is out. Right?"

"Right. There is no power of entry to gather evidence for a crime if there is no complaint of assault. The girl isn't going to cooperate. Is she?"

Grant shook his head. He should be annoyed that Sharon Davis was unwilling to accuse Adkins of assault, but he understood her reasoning. Police officers could deal with confrontations, then go back to the safety of their own homes. People in Ravenscliffe had to live among the thieves and burglars. If they gave evidence against them, they were easy targets for intimidation. That was a lot to ask of a nineteen-year-old girl.

"What about entry to prevent a further breach of the peace? An officer—that's me—fears for the girl's safety. Forced entry to preserve life."

Ballhaus smiled but shook his head. "Good try, but the girl was taken away in the ambulance. Remember?"

Grant raised his eyebrows.

"I knew that. Could have been discharged after treatment, though."

"At the BRI? You kidding? Takes three hours just to get through triage."

Grant scratched his head since rubbing his chin hadn't worked. Then he stopped and clicked his fingers.

"Okay. Evidence of an assault at the rugby club. Officer—that's me again—believes a crime has been committed that will only be disproved when Davis declines after treatment. Officer has reason to believe that Adkins committed that crime"—he held up the sealed evidence bag with the bloodstained bus pass in it—"and pursued the suspect to his place of residence. Suspect goes into house and locks the door. The officer, in continued pursuit of the felon, forces entry in order to effect the arrest."

Ballhaus nodded his approval and finished the chain of evidence.

"After making a lawful arrest, search of any premises that the prisoner has control over is allowed to preserve evidence for that crime."

Grant pointed at the SOCO under the sink.

"Including blood on the towel and in the sink."

Ballhaus smiled.

"Eureka."

Grant held up a hand. He wasn't finished yet.

"And during that search, evidence is uncovered of other crimes, namely drugs and money pertaining to illegal supply of Class A drugs."

Now that they'd got their story straight, Ballhaus stepped onto the landing and nodded towards the bathroom.

"You know, if you fell in a pile of shit, you'd come up smelling of roses."

Grant squeezed past the burly shift sergeant and stood in the bathroom doorway. The SOCO had almost finished with the sink. Now it was time to draw his attention to the bath panel.

IT TOOK OVER AN hour before drug squad detectives arrived at the house and took over. By that time SOCO had photographed the contraband in situ. Standard shots of the bath with the panel partly open, then with the panel removed. Then establishing shots of the sheer scale of the discovery followed by close-ups of the individual bags of white powder and rolled-up banknotes.

There were six large sealed bags of white powder, like five-pound bags of sugar only you wouldn't want it in your tea. Behind the bags was a cardboard tray containing 150 dealer bags, little self-sealed plastic baggies with individual portions ready for sale. Beside the tray were twenty-five thick rolls of ten-pound notes held together by elastic bands.

Twenty-five thousand pounds, it would turn out later.

The lead detective looked excited but weary. There was hours of work ahead seizing and labeling the evidence. Counting the money. Weighing the drugs. Making sure that the chain of evidence was observed. SOCO would have to fingerprint the bath and the panel. The bags would have to be removed and examined. They wouldn't bother with the money. Everyone who'd ever handled the banknotes would have left a trace.

This was a big find for a council estate. The value of the drugs would far outstrip the quantity of money they'd recovered. The rest of the house would have to be searched just in case there was more, but Grant told the lead detective there wouldn't be any. Adkins kept the house spotless for just that reason—so that no visiting police officers could stumble across his stash by accident while harassing the local villain. Grant should know. He'd been harassing Adkins for over a year.

The blue lights in the cul-de-sac thinned out. The rest of the shift went back to chasing the radio calls. Grant had a quiet word with his probationer. The only thing that Hope needed to be clear about was the continued pursuit from the rugby club to the house, which wasn't a stretch since Grant had come straight here after they'd taken the report. He left Hope watching the evidence being gathered in the bathroom and joined Ballhaus, who was still waiting in the front bedroom. The sergeant appeared to be having more fun than a shift supervisor normally got on a half-night tour.

Grant stood beside his sergeant in front of the window. "Like they used to say in *The A-Team*."

Ballhaus followed Grant's train of thought. "I love it when a plan comes together."

The only thing Ballhaus was missing was a big fat cigar.

Grant let out a sigh. "Thanks, Sarge. It's nice to know the good guys get to win now and again."

Ballhaus was about to reply, then his face stiffened.

"Thumb-up-the-arse brigade."

Grant followed his gaze through the window.

"What the fuck's he doing here?"

Down in the cul-de-sac an unmarked Astra pulled up behind Grant's patrol car. A tall, well-dressed man got out and strode towards the house. D&C's top bulldog, Inspector Nelson Carr. With two gold fillings in his false smile.

The question was, what was Discipline and Complaints doing at the scene of a routine drug seizure?

23:45 HOURS

"DIDN'T KNOW YOU COULD find your way around after dark."

Grant opened the front door before Carr made it all the way down the path. The lawn and flower borders were overgrown and full of weeds. Grant reckoned that Inspector Carr was a weed in the police force's garden—the sort of thing that grew unchecked if you didn't keep it down. The trouble was Grant was a police constable and Carr, an inspector. Carr tapped imaginary pips on his shoulder as a reminder.

"Sir."

Grant folded his arms across his chest. "Didn't know you could find your way around after dark. Sir."

Ballhaus stood behind Grant but couldn't see through the doorway. Grant felt his presence sending out a psychic message: *When you're up to your neck in shit, don't make waves.* The sergeant had no more love for D&C than any other policeman. They didn't call it the Rat Squad in America for nothing. Internal Affairs. At least in the UK they weren't quite so aggressive.

Not all of them.

"You need to remember you're not in the army now, PC Grant. There are rules."

"There were rules in the army. Sir. They just made better sense."

"The rules of engagement are different in the police service."

"Who's talking about rules of engagement?"

The D&C inspector stood with one foot on the doorstep and gave Grant his best hard stare. Grant had been stared at by harder men than Carr. With more serious consequences too. Carr stuck his jaw out as if that made the stare more devastating.

"What rules do you mean, then?"

Grant was about to relate the rule of brotherhood but knew it would sail right over the inspector's head. The bond that troops shared was the same as what frontline police enjoyed. It seemed to Grant that once bosses left the trenches and began to climb the career ladder, comradeship was the first thing they forgot. There was no point trying to explain.

"The QWERTY rule."

"What?"

"You've read my file. I was a typist."

Carr snorted a laugh. "Read your file? Damn thing's never off my desk. And here I am again, looking into your shit."

When you're up to your neck in shit, don't make waves. Apart from some creative writing, Grant felt he was on pretty firm ground tonight. This was a righteous drug bust that would take one of the major players off the streets for many years. Maybe not high stakes on the international stage but good by Ravenscliffe standards and good for the poor bastards who lived here. That should make the bosses happy. Unless you were a boss from Internal Affairs.

Carr let a hint of a smile play across his lips. Light glinted off his gold fillings. "Well, you fucked up this time."

Grant stood in the doorway and waited. You can't defend yourself until you know what the accusations are. Carr appeared to be enjoying himself. He took his time before continuing.

"Adkins didn't even make it through prisoner reception. He had a relapse in the ambulance. Broken ribs punctured his lung."

THE SHIFT SERGEANTS' OFFICE at Ecclesfield Police Station wasn't the perfect place for a discipline interview, but it would have to do. The nightshift inspector's office was busy with the handover from late turn to night duty. The sergeants' office would normally be busy too as the night staff prepared for briefing, but tonight wasn't a normal night. Inspector Carr commandeered the office, and nobody argued.

Sergeant Ballhaus closed the door behind him and sat in the far corner. Grant had the right to have a Police Federation rep present but said that his shift sergeant would do fine. He trusted Ballhaus over most people. Carr looked uncomfortable having such an experienced officer acting as witness. Grant didn't mind making the inspector feel uncomfortable.

The first thing Carr did was log onto the computer and bring up the Command and Control log for the rugby club disturbance. The IBIS system showed everything the radio operator had reported, including the times and call signs of any units deployed. The unit in question tonight was Alpha Two. Carr looked at the deployment sheet from the late turn briefing. Alpha Two was PC Grant and his probationer, PC Hope.

"You do not have to say anything, but it may harm your defence if you do not mention when questioned something which you later rely on in court. Anything you do say may be given in evidence."

Carr read the caution out loud even though the interview wasn't being recorded. Grant exercised his legal rights and said nothing. Ballhaus leaned backwards in his chair and waited. That put all the pressure back on the D&C inspector. He turned away from the computer and opened Grant's complaints file. It was a thick file. Rule of thumb was that a good policeman should have at least two complaints from the crooks he arrested per year, otherwise he wasn't doing his job properly. Anyone with a clean sheet must have spent his service never leaving the station. If you don't arrest anybody, then there's nobody to complain how you abused their rights.

Grant had arrested plenty of crooks. He had acquired much more than two complaints per year over the last twelve years. Upsetting the criminal fraternity was almost as much fun as making Inspector Carr feel uncomfortable. The inspector made a show of skimming through the file, but what he had to say wasn't in there. Instead he closed the file and referred to a printed sheet lying next to it.

"Let's review the evidence, shall we?"

Grant resisted the urge to ask if Carr was auditioning for David Frost's role in *Through the Keyhole*. He said nothing. Carr glanced at the sheet, then back at Grant. He ticked off each item on his fingers.

"Blood recovered from the U-bend will be tested and is expected to be from Sharon Davis."

That was one finger.

"Blood on the recovered towel. Ditto."

Two fingers.

"The bus pass that you recovered at the scene belongs to Adkins."

Three.

"And the blood on the bus pass is expected to be from Davis."

Four. He stopped using his fingers and simply told the story.

"That would suggest that Adkins was at the scene during the assault, but he could argue he'd lost the bus pass earlier and it just happened to be on the ground when she was assaulted. The blood on his hands, on the towel, and in the sink is more damning evidence and would certainly be enough to secure a conviction if the victim were to endorse the allegation of assault. Her injuries make it a Section 47, and therefore he could do prison time."

Carr paused for effect before continuing.

"Except the girl has not made a complaint, and there is no crime recorded."

He paused again, waiting for Grant to state the obvious—that a constable only needed to believe that a crime had been committed in order for his powers to be lawful. Good interview technique by Carr. Most people when confronted with silence during an interview felt the need to speak. Grant said nothing. Carr filled the void himself.

"But, of course, you had sufficient grounds to suspect a crime had been committed and that Adkins had committed it. You were therefore within your rights to seek him out."

Grant noted that the inspector didn't say *pursue*. He kept quiet.

Carr went back to using his fingers.

"Now. The other matter. During the struggle a bath panel was dislodged."

That was one finger.

"Items behind the panel were clearly visible."

That was two.

"Giving you reason to believe another crime had been committed and the authority to arrest Adkins for that offence and conduct a search of the premises."

Three. He gave up using the fingers early this time.

"The search was conducted in the presence of a Scenes of Crime Officer, who photographed the recovered drugs and cash in situ before examining the scene for fingerprints. Several latent prints were found on the inside of the bath panel and are expected to belong to Lee Adkins. Adkins is the sole occupant of the premises and therefore cannot claim the drugs were put there by somebody else."

Carr pushed back from the desk and swung the chair to face Grant.

"Drug Squad have taken over the investigation and expect the quantities, dealer bags, and cash to be enough to convict Adkins of supplying Class A drugs in such volume that he will be given a substantial prison sentence when the case goes to court."

Carr rested his hands in his lap and paused again. Grant wanted to wipe the smug expression off the inspector's face because he knew Carr was simply waiting to spring his trap. Grant said nothing. Carr couldn't keep quiet.

"That would make this an exceptional piece of police work leading to a known target being removed from society for a very long time."

Carr put his fingertips together and forced them upwards until his hands came together as if in prayer.

"But, like I said before, you fucked up this time."

He leaned forward and put added menace into his voice.

"Because the forced entry was illegal. And any evidence discovered inside the house is inadmissible."

THE ROOM FELL SILENT. Grant said nothing. His calm exterior belied the inner turmoil that Carr had just instilled in him. His mind raced through the facts and knew that the D&C inspector couldn't prove any of them to be false. Like anything else in the police service, it wasn't what you knew or suspected, it was what you could prove. Carr couldn't prove that Grant hadn't pursued Adkins to his house. That meant that Grant had legal authority to force entry in pursuit so long as he believed Adkins to be in the house.

Ballhaus sat up in his chair.

"Beggin' yer pardon, Inspector, but the chain of events supports Grant's story."

Carr ignored the sergeant, concentrating on Grant. "And that's exactly what it is, isn't it? A story. Just like all those other stories you've told over the years to get out of trouble."

Grant couldn't keep quiet any longer. He slouched in his chair and crossed one leg over the other to form a barrier between him and the inspector.

"You mean all the trouble caused by arresting more people than Sherlock Holmes? And those arrested persons being pissed off at the arresting officer? That the trouble you're talking about?"

Carr's eyes lit up at getting the bite.

"Good policemen do the job right. They don't need to piss people off."

Grant forced himself to remain calm. "The only way to not piss thieves off is to let them go."

"That is not true. I never pissed thieves off."

As soon as he spoke, he knew he'd made a mistake. Grant let the cock-up hang in the air for a few moments before responding.

"Point proved." Then he uncrossed his legs and leaned forward. "The only people you piss off are coppers trying to do their jobs."

Carr regained his composure. "Coppers breaking the rules to make the job easier. I am on to you, PC Grant. I will be on your case until the end of your career."

It was the inspector's turn to lean forward.

"And I will see to it that the end is nigh."

Ballhaus spoke from the corner of the room. "And I will give a statement saying that you are browbeating an officer who is just trying to lock up the pond life."

Carr sat back in his chair. "PC Grant is pond life. And I will end his career."

Grant kept quiet. Ballhaus didn't. "Not tonight, you won't."

Carr glanced at the sergeant and then back to Grant.

"Perhaps not. With twelve years' service, you will be a hard man to winkle out. We should have got you before your probation was up. The first two years. All I would have needed then was show you were unsuitable and"—he snapped his fingers—"you'd be gone."

Grant kept a poker face. "But I'm not in my probation. Am I?"

Carr let out a sigh. There was no getting around that. He appeared to consider what to do next before speaking again. "No, you're not, are you?"

He picked up the phone and dialed a number. When the call was answered, he spoke once—"send him in"—then hung up. He waited until footsteps approached the door.

"But somebody else is."

The door opened and Jamie Hope stepped into the office. His eyes were wide with fear. Grant's shoulders sagged.

00:20 HOURS

Ballhaus had to stand behind Grant as the constable put his baton and handcuffs away. Grant secured the grey metal locker and handed the keys to his sergeant. Ballhaus had already taken Grant's CS spray and the armory key, gas canisters being classed as Section 1 firearms for storage purposes. Grant rested his forehead against the cool metal and drummed his fingers on the locker door. When he regained his composure, he stood back and faced his sergeant.

"Don't worry about it. It's not your fault."

Ballhaus looked deflated. "That CPS lawyer is an arse."

Grant smiled, but it wasn't convincing. "You've just described the Crown Prosecution Service in general."

"Bunch of arses. I agree."

"Thumb-up-the-arse brigade."

"Led by the biggest arse thumber of 'em all."

Grant nodded. "He can't help being a bastard, though. Inspector Carr just doesn't know who his father is, that's all."

Grant unfastened the epaulets from his uniform shirt, then shrugged into his creased leather coat. He unclipped the black tie and opened his top button, letting his neck breathe. He tugged at the white T-shirt that was tight around his throat beneath the shirt.

"Worst they can do is say I made a mistake in the timeline and didn't keep the radio updated. Nothing criminal about that. Forced entry in good faith."

Ballhaus let out a sigh.

"It's not that, Jim, and you know it."

Grant folded his tie into the same hand as the epaulets.

"You sound like Doc McCoy in *Star Trek*. 'It's life, Jim, but not as we know it.'"

Ballhaus got serious. "You know what I mean."

Grant nodded, dropping the levity form his voice. "I do."

"Adkins is going to walk because you bent the rules."

"No, Sarge. He's going to walk because I didn't cover my back. I should have left Hope at the rugby club and gone after Adkins on my own. Then there would have been no contradictions."

Ballhaus leaned back against the locker room wall.

"You're one of the best coppers I've ever worked with. More of a thief taker than Kisby and Habergham put together. But it's a different ballgame nowadays. There are too many people looking to trip us up."

"Too many people with their thumbs up their arse."

"Agreed. It's more difficult to get crooks off the streets than before."

"Job's fucked."

Ballhaus laughed.

"The old guard were saying that when I joined. No doubt Jamie Hope will be saying it in twenty years. Change is never for the better. Not in the police service."

Grant stood to his full height and towered over the stocky sergeant.

"Slap on the wrist and a two-week suspension. Not guilty, your honor. Just make sure they don't burn Jamie."

Ballhaus slapped Grant on the back and looked away. Grant didn't think his sergeant believed he'd be back. CPS dropping the charges against Adkins was bad enough, but the punctured lung was more of a problem. Grant knew he hadn't done that but when it came to D&C, proof worked in reverse. Grant had to prove himself innocent. He put a brave face on it.

"Don't worry. I'll be back."

"Now who sounds like that *Star Trek* fella?"

"Sarge. Don't ever enter a pub quiz. You're thinking of Schwarzenneger in *The Terminator*. Except he didn't say 'don't worry,' just 'I'll be back.'"

"Fuck off, Jim. Who said that one?"

"You gonna escort me off the premises?"

"Not if you need a private moment."

Grant nodded.

"If you don't mind."

Ballhaus jerked his head towards the door.

"He's in the report room."

Jamie Hope looked as if the world had collapsed on his shoulders when Grant entered the constables' report-writing room, the place where they did the paperwork relating to any court file. Making an arrest was like taking a shit: the job wasn't finished until the paperwork was done.

Hope looked up at the sound of the door.

"I am so sorry. I really am."

Grant waved him not to get up and sat on the edge of the desk.

"Don't be daft. It's not your fault. I shouldn't have put you in that position."

"No, but—Christ. I fucked up."

Grant shook his head. "No, you didn't. I did. Broke one of the cardinal rules."

Hope looked nonplussed. Grant put one foot up on the chair and leaned his elbows on his knee. "Always cover your back. Make sure there's nothing they can prove against you."

"They couldn't have proved anything if I'd—"

Grant held up a hand.

"I'm supposed to be your tutor. Should be teaching you straight down the line. Once you've got your two years in and you're safe, then I can show you the ropes. Until then, they've got a lot of leverage."

"I want to lock crooks up."

"You will. Got to keep your job long enough first, though. What did I tell you about stab vests?"

Hope smiled. "They cover both sides for the bosses stabbing you in the back."

"That's right." Grant tapped his own back. "Case in point. Look and learn."

He stood up from the desk and went over to the shelves along the back wall containing blue plastic trays. He pulled out the one with his name on it and dropped his tie and epaulets on top of the ongoing enquiries that he'd been assigned. The sergeant would have to reallocate the crimes on his workload or extend their due-by date until he was back on duty. He pushed the tray closed and turned back to Hope.

"Don't stick your head above the parapet until you know it's safe."

"What?"

"Keep a low profile until you've got enough experience to know how to slant things in your favor."

Hope looked confused. Grant waved a calming hand.

"Never lie, just avoid giving a straight answer. Like when you're updating a burglary report with the house-to-house enquiries even though half the occupants were out. Rubber-stamp squad won't write it off unless every neighbor is accounted for. So be vague. Say, 'Enquiries made at houses three doors either side of the address,' not which house numbers you actually spoke to somebody at. Vague. If they find out you didn't speak to somebody, you can argue you never said you did. Just left a note for them to call back if they saw anything."

Hope nodded. "I'll remember that. But you'll be back soon, won't you?"

Grant thought about lying but decided to take his own advice. "We'll see. I know what I need now, though."

Hope glanced at his watch. "She working the nightshift again?"

"A drink. Doesn't matter who's working."

He patted Hope on the shoulder and went to the door. Before he opened it, he turned back to his probationer.

"And don't forget what I said earlier. Don't go waving your warrant card at a shitstorm when you're off-duty. Shitstorms never cease and desist. Best way to get the shit kicked out of you."

He took one last look around the report room. The wall clock showed it was half past twelve. It looked like this was one night when he hadn't survived the ruins of midnight, the time when most shit hits the fan. He raised a hand towards Hope, then walked out. He was halfway along the corridor before the door clicked shut.

SMOKE DRIFTED OUT PAST the No Smoking sign near the dog kennels in the back yard—the traditional smoking place since the bosses had declared the station a smoke-free zone. At least the dogs couldn't make a complaint, so it was the only place left for a crafty drag on duty. Grant ignored the smoke as he walked across the yard towards his car. He didn't feel like explaining why he was leaving early.

It was cold. A chill breeze made it even colder despite the secure yard being an enclosed space. Grant looked up at the sky and watched heavy clouds scurry across the darkness. Moonlight spilled into the yard from breaks in the cloud. A dog barked, maybe in response to the secret smoker.

Grant fished the car keys out of his pocket.

Then the smoker called him over.

He thought about ignoring the request but went over to the kennels anyway. Inspector Carr took one last drag, then stubbed the cigarette butt out on the floor. The security light glinted off his gold fillings.

"Sergeant Ballhaus is supposed to escort you off the premises."

"Didn't need to. I know the way."

"That's not the point. I trust he took your PPE."

"Trust? Doesn't sound like you."

"Your personal protective equipment. Handed it in?"

"Only backstabbing pencil pushers call it PPE. If you mean my gas, cuffs, and baton, yes, I've handed them in."

Carr grinned, his gold fillings catching the light again. "Warrant card?"

Grant took one step closer to the D&C inspector. "I've been suspended, not sacked. I keep my warrant card."

Carr took one step backwards to preserve his personal space. "For now."

Grant struggled to keep his anger in check. To remain calm on the outside despite being pissed off on the inside. He wasn't completely successful as he took another step towards Inspector Carr.

"For always. And if I find out you've gone after PC Hope, they won't find your teeth with a metal detector."

Carr backed up against the wall. Grant pointed at the No Smoking sign behind the inspector's head. "You're pretty selective about which rules to enforce, aren't you?"

Grant stuck his chin out.

"Well, I'm not. Touch him, and I'll fuck you up. With no witnesses."

Grant turned away and set off towards his car. He pressed the remote on the key fob and unlocked the doors. An electronic beep echoed through the yard. The Ford Mondeo's warning lights flashed twice. He was opening the driver's door when Carr shouted from the safety of distance.

"Still protecting the weak, eh, Grant?"

Grant held the door open but threw one final glance at the inspector.

"Still backing my colleagues. You should try it sometime."

He climbed into the driver's seat as the first flakes of snow drifted out of the darkness. The smoke pluming around Carr's head was his breath this time as he cast a farewell barb.

"Enjoy your holiday."

Grant shut the door and started the engine. He swung out of the parking bay and drove past the petrol pump. The heavy gate began to slide open in the headlight beams. When it cleared the exit he pulled forward, then waited for it to close behind him. Despite being suspended, the old habits died hard: never leave the station with the gate still open. The realization that he was a copper right down to his socks made him feel sad. The realization that tonight he was no longer a policeman. There was only one place to mourn that, so he turned left out of the driveway and headed into the night.

00:50 HOURS

GRANT WAS PISSED OFF long before he got to Snake Pass. Before the snow got heavier and the entire world decided to shoot it out at the Woodlands Truck Stop and Diner. He was pissed off but managing to cope with it. The prospect of a late night cup of tea with Wendy Rivers was the main reason why. It was also the reason he drove so far out of his way before pulling into the twenty-four-hour diner.

His headlights swept across the empty car park and picked out the front of the Yorkshire services renowned for aping its American counterparts. Woodlands Truck Stop wasn't a traditional motorway service station because the A57 wasn't a motorway. The winding road from Manchester to Sheffield that used to be the main route through the hillside forests was just a single-lane blacktop. There was no point using it after midnight and no good reason to have an all-night café sitting in the folds of the Yorkshire countryside. The upside was that Grant would have Wendy Rivers to himself.

He parked in the middle of the potholed tarmac facing the diner and turned the engine off. He waited a few minutes while he looked through the windows. There were no customers inside. The neon sign showed there were no other vehicles in the car park. The waitress and the chef lived in the next village down the valley and got dropped off for their night shift by the local taxi. The chef must be in the back somewhere because the only person Grant could see was Wendy Rivers busying herself behind the serving counter.

Grant closed his eyes and let out a lung-emptying sigh. He rubbed his temples with gloved fingertips and let his breathing settle into a normal rhythm. The long drive had given his troubles distance, but it was the thought of a peaceful half-hour with his favorite waitress that relaxed him. There was no value in getting angry with D&C. The internal structure of the police force was simply there to add weights and balances to the law. Bad cops needed bringing to book. It was a pity the likes of Inspector Carr focused on good cops bending the rules to get the job done.

He grunted a laugh, cleared his head with a shake, then opened his eyes. The best way to put your troubles behind you is to always look forward. What Grant was looking forward to was a drink and a chat with the dark-haired maiden with the piercing eyes. He got out of the car and slammed the door. Dodging puddled craters in the unkempt car park, he pressed the auto lock on his key fob and the Mondeo's lights blinked twice. The distinctive double beep sounded behind him. Rivers looked up from what she was doing.

"I THOUGHT COPS WENT for a beer after their shift."

"Coppers. You're not in America now."

"If I was back in America, it would be donuts."

"Is that right—the donuts thing? Always thought that was just in the pictures."

"Movies. And on TV. Most cops in the US weigh two-fifty, three hundred pounds. And it's not all muscle."

"Most coppers here weigh the same—in stones, not pounds. Mainly beer."

Rivers put the steaming mug of tea on the counter. "You don't."

"Give me time. The weight usually piles on around the same time they get all bitter and twisted."

She pushed the mug towards Grant's barstool. "You don't seem bitter and twisted either."

"Hidden depths. You'll have to get to know me better first."

Rivers leaned her elbows on the counter and rested her head on her hands. "How am I going to get to know you better? You only ever come round in the middle of the night."

"Only time I can guarantee catching you without customers."

"You got that right. They don't call this the graveyard shift for nothing."

Grant shifted on his seat and took a swig of tea. It was too hot and he had to blow it first. Steam wafted across the counter. He glanced over Rivers's shoulder towards the kitchen.

"Who's the Master Chef tonight?"

"Mickey. He's back there sharpening his knives or something."

"Safest place for me then. Out here."

"Safest place for me too. Having the po-lice here to protect me."

"I'm off-duty."

"So?"

"So if anybody comes to rob you, give 'em the money. I don't get involved when I'm off-duty."

The assertion brought Jamie Hope to mind, and Grant felt a wave of sadness wash over him. He'd been a policeman for twelve years and spent eight years in the army before that. He was a dyed-in-the-wool uniformed protector. Being suspended put him in limbo: neither one thing nor the other. No police powers and no protective equipment. No radio and no backup. Rivers brought him out of his reverie.

"They're not gonna get much out of the night till."

"No reason not to give 'em it, then."

"What about the principle, though? Isn't right, them taking what isn't theirs."

"It isn't yours either."

"That doesn't make it right."

"Right's got nothing to do with it. We can always catch 'em later. First order of business is to protect yourself: don't resist, don't argue. Give it up."

Rivers lowered her voice and leaned forward. "Is that what you'd suggest? Just give it up?"

Grant paused with the mug halfway to his lips. He put it down on the counter and smiled. He reckoned there must be some chemical reaction connected to smiling because whenever he did, he felt happier. It often worked in his favor during confrontational situations too. People usually felt less inclined to hit you if you were smiling at them. Wendy Rivers didn't look like she was planning on hitting him. He nodded at his steaming mug.

"I hope you're not like this with all the customers."

"Like what?"

"All submissive."

"Like with handcuffs and suchlike?"

"And suggestive."

"I don't know what you mean."

Grant pushed back from the counter and stood up. He wafted a hand in front of his face. "Is it just me or is it getting warm in here?"

Rivers stepped back and waved at the hotplates bubbling under the lights. "Gets a bit like a sauna in here sometimes. Even without any food to serve."

Grant walked to the front of the diner and opened a small top window. The burst of fresh air lowered the temperature. He'd been coming to see Wendy Rivers for almost six months and had no intention of moving things forward. He wasn't in the right place to spark up another friendship at the moment. All he wanted was sex and solitude. Putting the move on somebody he liked would compromise the simplicity of that lifestyle.

He went back to the counter and changed the subject. "Don't know how they manage to keep open if it's not taking money."

Rivers accepted the tactful rebuttal. She waved a hand to include everything around her. "Place is a beacon in the night. Never closes. Never goes out."

"Never makes any money."

Rivers shrugged. "Must make enough during the day and at weekends. Hikers and tourists. And it's not like they pay the night staff a fortune."

Grant drank his tea. It had cooled enough for big gulps now. "You could do better elsewhere."

The waitress shrugged again. "It serves a purpose. Peace and solitude in the night. Sometimes we all need a little bit of that. I'm low maintenance."

Grant put the mug down. "And I'm a cheap date."

Their eyes locked, and he was reminded of just how beautiful she was. Dark Hispanic features. Unruly black hair. Piercing brown eyes. Full lips and high cheekbones with very little makeup. He had to question why he'd never asked her out. It wasn't like he'd been celibate since the main woman in his life had gone. A brief flash of another pair of eyes and a different smile ran through his mind. A dusty army combat suit and a swaying stethoscope. The picture vanished as quickly as it had appeared, and then he was simply smiling at a beautiful woman in a roadside diner.

"And I need the toilet."

Rivers laughed. It always ended up this way. A bit of flirting. Some suggestive comments. Then Grant beating a hasty retreat, this time to the restroom. She pointed to the illuminated sign at the far end of the restaurant.

"Don't forget to wash your hands before you come back."

Grant nodded and gave her a little wave. He had no intention of coming back. He'd had his flirtation fix for the night, and the bad taste that his confrontation with D&C had left was gone. Smiling at Inspector Carr would never work. At least smiling with Wendy Rivers had done its job and ended his night on a good note instead of a sour one.

He walked into the shadows. The serving counter and main section was only part lit. The gents' toilets had a side door into the car park. That was Grant's exit strategy. He threw a farewell comment that he knew Rivers would recognize as a farewell comment.

"And don't forget to give 'em the money. Don't be a hero."

Rivers raised her voice over the bubbling hotplates. "That's your job, remember?"

"Not tonight. I'm off-duty. Thanks for the drink."

Her shouted "you're welcome" was cut off by the toilet door swinging closed. Grant went into the first cubicle on the left, wondering if he showed his warrant card, would Wendy Rivers cease and desist?

The snowflakes were getting bigger as Grant crossed the car park to his Mondeo, but they still weren't settling. The ground was too wet and the potholed tarmac too puddled with standing water. There was a thin skein of white across the level parts, though, and the temperature was dropping. It wouldn't be long before the sleet became real snow and the roads became icy.

He used the key instead of the central locking to avoid the double beep and flashing lights. When making a tactful withdrawal it didn't do to telegraph what you were doing. He unlocked the door and sagged into the driver's seat. The internal light went off after he'd closed the door, and he sat for a few minutes looking out across the cold, wet tarmac. The thin white layer had become deep enough to show his dark wet footprints coming from the side of the diner. They were beginning to fill in already.

The lights behind the serving counter stood out against the darkness of the car park. Grant sat and watched as Rivers washed his cup and put it away. Steam drifted into the night air from an aluminium chimney above the kitchen. It hung against the dark, surrounded by falling snowflakes. There was no breeze. The steam didn't move. The snow fell straight with barely any deviation. The night was motionless apart from the waitress moving around inside.

Something caught Grant's eye.

Not his footprints filling with snow but longer, wider marks that also stood out against the white. Tire tracks sweeping across the car park around the left-hand side of the diner. He looked at Rivers standing behind the counter and saw her head jerk towards her right. Then the dining-area lights went out, and the neon car park sign blinked off.

01:25 HOURS

THE LIGHTS NEVER WENT out at the Woodlands Truck Stop and Diner. It was a beacon in the night. Rivers had said it, and Grant knew it. He'd driven past here at all hours of the night, and it had never been closed. Now the car park was in darkness, the interior lit only by the serving counter light. Grant felt himself relax—a sure sign that there was trouble ahead.

Rivers was talking. Grant could see her mouth forming words that didn't look friendly. He scoured the shadows where she was looking but couldn't see any movement. Rivers threw the tea towel down on the counter and spoke again. She waved a hand in a get-out-of-here gesture. Probably a get-the-fuck-out-of-here instruction. Whomever she was talking to didn't appear to be complying because the next words she spoke were shorter and louder. He could tell by the muscles straining in her neck.

Grant watched and waited.

Rivers stuck her jaw out and put her hands on her hips, defiance written all over the pose. When she spoke this time, she jerked her head towards the car park. Grant shook his head. He hoped she wasn't threatening the intruders with the police officer sitting outside. Then she pointed at the front door. No, she wasn't. She was telling them to get out. Good. The less they knew about Grant, the better. If this was just some late-night ruffians causing trouble, he had no doubt that Rivers could handle them. Diffusing troublesome drinkers was one of her skill sets. He'd seen her do it before with a smile and a jaunty aside. She wasn't smiling tonight.

Grant continued to watch, then saw why.

Two men walked through the dining area towards the counter. As they came out of the shadows, their size and demeanor emphasized the threat. They were tall and lean and built like rugby players. Broad shoulders. Thick necks. Strong, aggressive movements. That was bad enough. Difficult to talk down, even for Wendy Rivers. What set them apart from every other drunk she'd had to deal with were the black balaclavas pulled down over their faces and the baseball bats they each held loosely in their hands.

Grant flexed his shoulders. This wasn't a drunken prank; it was a robbery. He focused on the two big fellas, then glanced at Rivers. He tried to send a message. *Don't argue. Just give 'em the money.* The leading robber pointed at the till on the end of the counter. Rivers backed off a pace.

"Give 'em the money."

His voice was a whisper, but the message got through. Rivers stepped forward and pressed a couple of buttons, then the cash drawer flew open. *Good girl.* The first man walked around the counter to the open drawer. Grant flicked his eyes to the side of the diner. He could just make out exhaust fumes hanging in the cold night air, but no lights. Whatever getaway vehicle they were using, the engine was running. The question was, did they leave it running when they went in or was there a driver waiting for them to come out?

Don't go wading in without communication or backup. Off-duty is off-duty.

His warning to Jamie Hope seemed hollow and pointless now, but Grant knew they were sensible words. He reminded himself that he was not only off-duty but, strictly speaking, he wasn't even a policeman anymore. His powers throughout England and Wales had been suspended. *This isn't exactly the great train robbery. Let it slide. Or, if you feel strongly, tell the store detective.*

Grant continued to watch the scenario through the diner window to make sure things remained calm. This wasn't a supermarket theft so he couldn't tell the store detective. What he could do was call the police. Keeping his eyes on Wendy Rivers, he opened the glove compartment and scrabbled around for his mobile phone. His fingers discounted the window squeegee and the screen wipes, then scampered over a tin of extra-strong mints. He had to look down for a second to find the phone at the back of the drawer and pick it up.

He brushed off the dust and crumbs of mint. He wasn't big on technology. Owning a mobile phone was just a nod towards moving with the times, but he didn't carry it with him and hardly ever used it. It was turned off. Shit. Grant pressed the on button and waited for the phone to cycle through its power-up menus.

Grant checked the diner. The first robber was emptying the cash drawer into his pocket. The second had moved past him and was talking to Rivers. Outside, the exhaust fumes plumed around the back of the getaway car.

The phone beeped. Grant brought it towards his face with both hands. He hadn't mastered the one-handed technique. The screen was blinking. He tried to remember if he had to enter a pin number, then realized he hadn't programmed the security menu. He looked for the signal strength bar in the top corner. It wasn't there. The screen was blank except for a flashing battery symbol and a warning message. Then the phone died.

TIME FOR PLAN B, Grant told himself. Keep an eye on Rivers to make sure she was safe, but let the robbers get away and arrest them later. This was no time to go charging in waving his warrant card and telling them to cease and desist. Even if his warrant card still gave him authority throughout England and Wales, it didn't give him shit-all in a robbery with no baton and stab vest. Never get involved off-duty.

He was trying hard to convince himself, but it wasn't working. He was a dyed-in-the-wool uniformed protector. Sitting and watching wasn't in his nature. Trouble was, it was the only thing to do. He was out of uniform, and he no longer had the power of the West Yorkshire Police behind him. He couldn't arrest them, and he couldn't call for backup. This was Lone Ranger time. Shit or bust.

He'd almost talked himself into waiting the robbery out when the second robber upped the ante. Out in the car park, the snow was getting heavier. Inside the diner, the atmosphere was changing. The big fella lowered the baseball bat but swung up with his free hand. He smacked Rivers a backhanded blow across the face and changed the outcome of everything.

01:35 HOURS

Moments in time that change the course of history. Grant was aware such things existed but didn't dwell on the past enough to offer an opinion. He knew all that stuff about "because of a nail, a shoe was lost, leading to the horse, the battle, and the war being lost." If he were to look back on the course of his life later, however, there'd be no denying he'd just witnessed a life-changing moment in time. Some might argue that the true life-changing event was Grant slamming Lee Adkins's face into the sink, since that was the reason he'd been suspended and was parked outside the Woodlands Truck Stop and Diner in the first place, but Grant reckoned up to that point his future had been safe. He could survive a two-week suspension, then get back to work at Ecclesfield Police Station, no problem.

When the big fella in the ski mask slapped Wendy Rivers across the face, all that changed. If the robber had shown a bit more restraint, then everything that happened after might have been avoided. There would have been no death and no destruction at the truck stop, and Grant wouldn't have been sent to Jamaica Plain in America. So there was some good and some bad that came out of that single blow. Mainly bad.

Don't go wading in without communication or backup went out of the window immediately. Drunks fighting each other outside a Chinese takeaway was one thing, and stealing citric acid for your drug habit was easily forgivable, but hit a woman in the face and you'd better prepare to reap the whirlwind. His first instinct was to charge in and dish out some payback. *How do you like it, fuck-face?* Lee Adkins hadn't liked it at all. The big fella in the ski mask wouldn't like it either. Attacking out of anger was a bad tactical choice, though. Back in his army days, first instincts could get you killed.

Grant sat and waited. He saw Rivers roll with the blow but stay upright. She didn't offer any resistance. Good girl. The big fella wasn't provoked into a second strike. The first robber finished emptying the till. Grant scanned the shadowy interior for additional movement, but the diner was empty apart from the trio standing in the pool of light at the counter. The only other threat might come from the getaway driver. That was Grant's first consideration.

He reached up and flicked the interior light switch from auto to off, then opened the door. The Mondeo stayed dark. He got out and closed the door without making a noise. The three figures were still together inside the diner. Exhaust fumes still plumed around the getaway car on the left. Grant crossed the car park in a wide arc, keeping away from the pool of light that spilled from the diner windows. As he drew nearer to the exhaust fumes, he realized that the getaway car was a delivery van. There were no windows along the side and just two in the back doors. Either it was the only vehicle they could steal or they were planning on taking more than the money from the till.

Grant reached the back of the van and threw a quick glance in the rear windows. The interior was dark, but he could just make out the silhouette of the driver waiting to speed off. Just one man. Grant kept out of sight below the rear doors and considered his options. He could confront the driver and disable the van, but that would mean leaving the two big men with no escape. A cornered animal was the most dangerous game. He didn't want to put Rivers in any more danger than necessary. Best not to box them into a corner. Better to give them an easy out. He made a mental note of the van's registration number, then backed away, avoiding the sight lines from the rear-view mirrors.

He crossed the car park to the toilet door on the other side. He paused for a moment and listened at the door he'd come out of fifteen minutes ago. He could hear raised voices and some activity, but no more violence. The door opened with ease. Grant remembered it hadn't creaked before. He slipped inside and closed the door behind him. Now the voices were clearer. The men talking. Rivers keeping quiet. Good girl. She wasn't giving them any excuse to hit her again.

Grant kept to the shadows of the extended dining room, moving slowly from table to table, careful not to knock anything. He didn't crouch and he didn't bend over; he wanted to keep a strong base to attack from. Instead, he edged towards the wall and followed the line towards the counter, using the pillars and curtains for cover.

Both men had moved from the till and were emptying armloads of cigarettes from the display behind the counter into a cardboard box. The first man brought out a second box and began to fill that one too. Typical restaurant robbery. Take the money and cigarettes. If Woodlands had been licensed, they'd be stealing the wines and spirits too. Neither of them had removed their masks. That was a good sign. It meant they wanted to get away without their faces being seen. It also meant there was no need to disable the waitress.

Grant stopped at the edge of the shadows and pressed against the wall next to the serving tray stand. A long, hanging drape obscured his view. It was almost time to spook the stampede. He picked up a metal tray, keeping it behind his back so the light didn't reflect off the shiny surface. The plan was simple. Make plenty of noise as he crossed the open space and shout as loud as he could that he was the police. Most thieves when confronted by the police went in the opposite direction. Grant hadn't found a crook yet whose first instinct wasn't to get away. The van was outside the far door. Grant was coming from the right. It would be like herding sheep.

That was the plan.

Until the big fella fucked it up by hitting Wendy Rivers again.

THE SECOND BLOW DIDN'T come out of the blue.

"Where's the fuckin' safe?"

The big fella stepped in front of Rivers. Grant could see his eyes were fizzing with anger. Probably taken something to build himself up for the job. Local accent. Not well educated. Pond life. Grant had been dealing with his kind for twelve years. Safe crackers they were not. But he asked the question again.

"The fuckin' safe. Where's it at?"

Rivers looked stunned. "There isn't one."

The big fella jutted his chin forward. "Don't fuck me about, lady."

Then Rivers made her first mistake. Instead of keeping quiet, she tried to explain. "You've seen how much was in the till. What do we need a safe for?"

That was all the verbal confrontation he needed. Rivers was standing back and letting them take what they wanted. What the big fella obviously wanted was a bit more action. While his colleague continued filling a third box, he stepped forward and whipped a forehand slap across her face. The force of the blow knocked her off her feet, and she went down hard. Grant had met thieves like these before. The sort of burglars who weren't satisfied with stealing your money, they had to shit on your carpet as well. In this case, they just had to leave a little pain behind.

The first robber snapped his head up at the sound of the slap. The second was focused on Rivers falling to the ground. Neither was looking at the shadowy curtain along the side wall and didn't see the movement until it was too late.

Grant barged two tables out of the way, then vaulted over the counter next to the hotplates. He was balanced and moving as soon as he landed. He cocked one arm and flung the tray like a Frisbee. The silver disc flashed across the short distance and hit the first robber in the throat. He dropped the box and gasped for air. The big fella followed the flight of the silver tray with his eyes and was too slow to come round into a defensive position. Grant stamped on the outside of his front leg and collapsed it like a folding tripod. As the big fella went down, Grant slammed an elbow into his throat. Now they were both on the floor, clutching their windpipes.

Grant picked up the fallen baseball bats and cracked them together. The harsh smack of wood on wood made Rivers flinch. Grant ignored her for now and kicked the first robber in the ribs. He rolled over towards the door and tried to get up. Good. The second slap across Rivers's face hadn't changed Grant's initial plan—chase these thugs off and catch 'em later. To that end, he yanked both balaclavas off and kicked the second robber. He glared into their faces, memorizing every line.

No radio and no backup.

Discretion was the better part of valor.

Keeping an eye on the injured robbers, Grant moved towards Rivers. She was shaking and taking shallow breaths. Delayed shock. He helped her to her feet and guided her away from the intruders. Both men took the hint and scrambled to their feet. The big fella was limping but moved surprisingly fast. His accomplice gave him a shoulder to lean on, and they went out of the door in a hurry. Van doors slammed and the engine roared, then Grant was helping Rivers towards the sink to wash the blood off her face.

"I THOUGHT YOU SAID you were off-duty."

She winced as Grant dabbed cold water on her lip and nose. The nose looked sore but not broken. The lip was split and leaking blood. The entire side of her face was inflamed from being slapped. Grant held the sponge against her cheek for the coolness to ease the pain.

"I thought I said don't resist. Don't argue. Give it up."

She winced again. "I did give it up. There was nothing else to give."

"Then you should have kept it cool while they figured that out."

She took the sponge out of his hand and rinsed it under the cold tap. When she raised it back up to her face, she was staring at him.

"I did keep it cool."

"You said, 'What do we need a safe for?'"

"I said, 'You've seen how much was in the till. What do we need a safe for?' I was aiming for light and witty."

"Well, you missed by a country mile. That feel better?"

"No. But it's better without you pressing against it."

"Sorry. My medical expertise ends with aspirin and field dressings."

"Mine ends with blue plasters and Germolene."

Her bravado evaporated all at once, and she let out a sigh that bordered on tears. "Thank you."

"I didn't give you aspirin."

"For the other thing. Thanks for coming back."

"You're welcome. Like I said, we'll catch 'em later."

The words were barely out of his mouth when he realized that wasn't going to happen. The noise outside was unmistakable. Van doors bursting open. Not the driver's door but the doors at the rear. The two big fellas barged into the diner, followed by two others from the back of the van. None of them were wearing ski masks. They weren't bothered about being seen this time.

01:50 HOURS

GRANT WEDGED A CHAIR under the serving area door and snatched a knife from the magnetic strip on the wall. The food preparation area was a small room behind the counter for making sandwiches and cleaning up. It had a marble worktop, a double drainer sink, and nothing else. The door from the diner had a circular window. The door through to the back did not. There was no time to scout ahead.

"Come on."

He helped Rivers stand up from leaning over the sink but she wavered, her eyes blurring, then coming back to focus. The blows to the head must have knocked her off-kilter, and she needed help just standing straight. Not good for a fast getaway.

"You'll be okay."

An optimistic lie. If he didn't get her out of here fast, she'd be a long way from okay. The reassurance appeared to settle her because she shook her head clear and her eyes brightened. She nodded and followed Grant's lead towards the unmarked door in the back wall.

Then her stomach cramped, and she doubled over.

"I'm sorry" came out part apology and all vomit. She was sick on the floor. Doubling over took her below the window in the front door. Grant checked on the four intruders and ducked under the window too. They'd come halfway across the restaurant and spread out. The initial pair were coming straight for the counter. The other two had gone on either side of the serving area. Nobody seemed to be interested in the porthole into the back room. That gave Grant a few extra seconds.

He grabbed a tea towel from the counter and gave it to Rivers. She nodded her thanks and wiped her mouth, apologizing through the cloth. Grant wondered where Mickey Frevert was and how to warn him. The chef's kitchen was further along the front counter, with a serving hatch for delivering cooked meals to the waitress. He must be deaf not to have heard the commotion.

Grant couldn't worry about that now. His main concern was Rivers. He had to get her out of here before tackling the other problem. Four armed robbers, even if they were only armed with baseball bats. A baseball bat could cause serious damage. The straight-bladed kitchen knife helped level the playing field but not by much. He kept low and edged Rivers towards the back door. She was moving better but in no shape for a sprint to freedom.

A quick check through a gap he opened in the door was all he allowed himself, then he yanked it open and dragged Rivers into the corridor. Turn right and it would lead back into the dining area. Turn left and it was a home run past the storage rooms to the fire exit into the rear car park.

Grant turned left.

Rivers doubled over and was almost sick again. Grant held the towel over her mouth. He didn't want a trail of puke showing which way they'd gone. He kept his voice low.

"Hold on there. Hold on."

Rivers moaned into the towel.

She wasn't going to make the car park.

Grant scanned the corridor and made a snap decision. The storage rooms included a walk-in pantry and an industrial cooler that was like a refrigerator except it was the size of a small room. He could tell the difference by the doors. The fridge had a big metal affair with rubber seals and a cantilevered handle. The dry goods store opposite was a standard door but with an air vent at the top. He opened the pantry door and bundled Rivers inside.

The store was lined with wooden shelves from floor to ceiling. There were boxes and cans and bottles of everything the chef might need to knock out a selection of hot meals, depending on what the menu offered. There were also sacks of potatoes and barrels of cooking oil. Grant dropped to a crouch and scanned the bottom shelves for storage space.

"In there. And don't move."

Rivers took a deep breath. The color was returning to her face. She nodded and slid into the bottom shelf. Grant pulled some of the cardboard boxes in front of her and gave her the thumbs up. He cracked the door an inch and glanced back along the corridor. No movement, but he could hear banging from the kitchenette. They hadn't got through the blocked door yet.

Grant jogged to the end of the corridor. The sounds of hammering echoed down the hallway. Two enormous thumps against the door. Glass broke. Wood splintered. The chair or the doorframe or both. Angry voices shouted above the noise. All of it meant Grant could go out the back door without being heard. He strode down the corridor, passed a side hallway, and opened the door. He was about to charge round the side of the building when he stopped dead.

The snow wasn't heavy, but it had dusted the ground white.

Outbuildings jutted from the wall along the rear, and steam bloomed into the cold night air behind the generator exhaust. There was a wire enclosure for additional storage. Apart from that, there was no cover as far as the eye could see. In the dark, the eye could only see a few feet in any direction, but Grant saw enough to know that wherever he went he'd leave a trail of footprints.

There was no wind to drift the snow.

There were no vehicles parked round the back.

A loud crash sounded from the kitchenette. The angry voices grew louder. Time was up. Grant stepped into the dark and closed the door behind him.

SILENCE. THE THIN COVERING of snow and the falling flakes sucked all the sound out of the night. It reminded Grant of doing foot patrol in the early hours and soaking up the peace and quiet. He took a deep breath and let it out slow, the steam forming a cloud around his head.

Footsteps charged along the corridor. A verbal exchange that wasn't friendly. Then the fire exit door burst open and the two robbers shouldered each other out of their way, eager to grab the man who had laid them low. They didn't even notice the snow until after they'd scuffed an area six feet square around the door. When they did, it was a few seconds longer before they thought to check for footprints.

The only footprints were the confused stampede marks they'd made themselves. The first robber was the brightest of the pair. He was also the faster mover, not having to contend with the limp that was slowing his partner down. He scanned the ground beyond their little melee.

There was no trail to follow.

"He dint come this way. Back inside."

The man with the limp didn't need telling twice. It was freezing out here. He shuffled back through the door, and the other one threw a last glance across the car park before slamming the door. The footsteps receded, then turned left along the secondary hallway.

The night became quiet again.

The snow continued to fall.

Grant counted to five, then lowered his head down from the low overhang. The lip of the roof provided shelter for a two-foot strip along the back wall. Still conscious of leaving footprints, he stayed on the flat roof and followed the building line around the corner, towards the left side of the diner. Towards the Ford Transit van and the lone driver.

HE WASN'T GOING TO make the same mistake twice. The van might be their only means of escape, but the gang had already made their intentions clear. They weren't in any hurry to drive off into the night, so there was no need to leave them that option.

Grant kept low as he reached the corner of the building. An empty oil drum with its top cut off stood against the wall below him. A drainpipe from the guttering ran into the top. Woodlands Truck Stop and Diner used the barrel to save water for menial tasks. The barrel was the only cover along the side wall. The van was parked at an angle, pointing away from the diner, with its lights off. The only security light was above the fire exit round back. That meant Grant would be in shadow when he dropped down beside the barrel.

He slowed his breathing to limit the steam around his head.

The van's rear doors were open. Grant sidled along the edge of the roof to get a better view into the back of the Transit. He didn't want any more surprises. There was nobody else inside. It was obviously a stolen works van. Just a selection of tools and equipment and canvas sacking. The engine was still running. That meant the driver was still in the front seat. There was no sign of him from this angle, but Grant doubted the heavy mob would leave their flanks vulnerable or their getaway vehicle unprotected.

The drainpipe was plastic. The U-brackets and screws holding it to the wall were lightweight. Not solid enough to climb down. Grant listened. All the noise inside the diner had moved towards the kitchen and till area. Nobody was coming out front anytime soon. He concentrated on the van. The engine rumbled, and a hole in the exhaust let out a throaty roar every time the driver dabbed the accelerator. More than enough noise to cover Grant climbing from the roof. He swung his legs over the edge and hung at full stretch. His feet were only three feet from the ground. He let go and dropped into a crouch beside the oil drum. The rubber soles of his hi-tech Magnums didn't make a sound.

The snow hadn't gotten heavier, but a steady curtain of flakes now drifted from the sky. The constant movement meant the driver's eyes had grown accustomed to it, but Grant still had to be careful not to make sudden moves. Keeping low against the side of the building, he edged towards the back of the van, watching the driver's door all the way. He was checking to see if the door was unlocked. As the light shifted with his angle, he saw the button was popped up inside the door window. Good. The slack band of a seat belt hung loose against the window. Even better. The driver wasn't strapped in.

Grant kept the knife behind his back, away from the light.

Once he was past the driver's door, he stepped away from the building. Now that he was moving, he didn't stop. One sweeping charge and Grant came up alongside the driver, just behind the rear-view mirror. He yanked the door open and climbed up on the step to reach inside. Holding the knife as a threat, he took the slack of the seat belt and whipped it around the driver's neck, then pulled it tight. The driver let out a strangled yell that fizzled in his throat. Grant was ready to put all his weight behind the noose before he realized he was dealing with a midget.

The driver's face had gone red. His legs barely reached the pedals. They flapped in the footwell. No wonder he'd been elected the getaway driver. He was two feet shorter than the fellas doing the robbery. Grant held the seat belt tight and slipped the knife into the back of his trousers. He ran his hand over the driver's pockets but there were no weapons. All the baseball bats were in the diner.

This was no time to start feeling sorry for the little fella. Grant watched the driver's eyes bug out of his face until they went dull and he slumped forward before releasing the seat belt.

"You should have stuck with *Lord of the Rings,* you little fucker."

There was no response. Grant dropped to his knees and tugged the knife out of his belt. He shoved the blade into the front tire, then went round the van, slashing all four wheels. The van settled on the rims. As he passed the open rear doors, he spotted a pile of empty sacks and rolls of electric cable. He'd applied just enough pressure on the improvised chokehold to black the driver out, but he wouldn't stay unconscious for long. He smiled and jumped in the back of the van.

Five minutes later, the driver was tied up in a sack and being dragged towards the oil drum. Grant tipped it over to empty the water, then shoved the sack into the drum. He stood it back up against the wall, then headed for the front of the diner.

THE INTERIOR WAS STILL mainly in darkness. The robbers hadn't turned the rest of the lights on. Grant wasn't surprised. Armed robbery in the night might be a violent crime, but doing it in a brightly lit restaurant for anyone outside to see was still more than most robbers wanted to do. Thieves always preferred the shadows rather than the spotlight.

The big fella with the limp and his partner came back behind the counter. The other two had disappeared. Grant stood beside the brickwork between window frames and scanned the dining area. There was no sign of them. There was no sign of Wendy Rivers either. That gave him some relief. They hadn't found her.

He was considering his next move when a door farther along the serving counter opened and the other two robbers came out of the kitchen. A scrawny young man barely out of his teens was dragged out by the arms. His chef's whites were stained with blood from a blow to the face. His nose was bleeding, and one eye was swollen shut. The reason Mickey Frevert hadn't heard the commotion dangled from his collar. Blood trickled down his neck where the earphones had been yanked out of his ears. His face was as white as his smock.

Grant felt a shiver of foreboding run up his spine.

The two robbers held Frevert by the upper arms and stood him in front of the till. He had his back to the window, but Grant could sense the fear in him. He was babbling for them not to hurt him.

The words were lost in the snow swirling around Grant's head. He moved along the front windows until he was standing beneath the top-opener he'd opened earlier. Fresh air wasn't the issue now; hearing what was being said was.

He kept to the shadows and listened.

The first man to speak was the shorter of the two holding Frevert. He was still a tall man but held himself with more dignity. He spoke better than the fella who'd threatened Rivers. The local accent was more educated.

"Okay, master chef. How much do you want to keep your fingers?"

Frevert shook his head but didn't speak. How do you answer a question like that? The implied threat was enough because when the next question was asked, he answered straightaway.

"Where's the safe?"

"In the office. Floor safe. Under the desk."

"Very good."

Frevert developed verbal diarrhoea.

"There's a circle cut out of the carpet. You know—with a bit of carpet stuck in. Combination lock. Only a small thing. Buried into the concrete. Not big. But it's never used. All the money's in the till until they bank it during the day."

The leader patted Frevert on the shoulder. "Slow down. Relax. A combination lock?"

"Yes. But it's no use. There's no money in it."

The leader nodded and squeezed his fingers into the joint.

"Who said we're after money?"

02:05 HOURS

GRANT FELT THAT SHIVER of foreboding crawl up his neck again. Burglars and robbers were ten a penny in Yorkshire. They ranged from disgruntled teenagers to grizzled old timers. Their targets varied from domestic burglaries to corner shop robberies, but there was one thing they all had in common: they were always about the money or the cigarettes or the electronic equipment. More upscale robbers might be after the jewelry. Grant had never heard of a robber who wasn't interested in money.

He glanced across the car park at the Ford Mondeo. It was barely visible in the gloom beyond the diner lights. Then he looked at the Transit van, sitting like a broken-legged bug on its slashed tires. A stolen electrician's van. Not very upscale. This wasn't Raffles or The Great Train Robbers. These were local heavies. What could a floor safe in a struggling diner possibly contain that was of more interest than the cash they'd already stolen?

The leader clapped his hands. "Show me."

Frevert jerked his head up at the noise. "What?"

"The office safe. Show me where it is."

"But there's nothing—"

The next slap wasn't his hands clapping. The blow snapped Frevert's head to one side and knocked him backwards against the empty till. Grant felt his blood boil. He didn't restrict his protective instincts for damsels in distress. His mind raced as he tried to remember if he'd ever been to the office. He had. One time when he'd come to see Rivers, he'd needed to ring the station about a court file that needed submitting. Just to remind the CPS lawyer that it was in the custody suite. The office was round the back, along the secondary corridor he'd passed earlier. Above the boiler room in the cellar.

Two big men grabbed Frevert by the arms again. One limped along behind him. The fourth, who was really the top man, led the way as Frevert gave directions to the main hallway leading to the back. Grant was already rounding the corner of the building. He wanted to be down in the cellar by the time the entourage reached the office.

HE DIDN'T WORRY ABOUT leaving footprints this time. Grant sprinted round the end of the dining area and passed the side door near the toilets. He was mindful of passing the main windows but kept in a crouch until he was around the corner.

The rear of the complex was more utilitarian. More brickwork and timber than windows for the customers. The customers didn't get round the back here. He skirted the right-hand side of the building and approached the chainlink fencing from the opposite direction than when he'd gone out of the rear door. The generator exhaust pumped steam into the night. The exterior compound jutted out from the back wall. The stairs to the cellar were just this side of the compound.

Grant paused to catch his breath at the top of the stairs. They disappeared down into darkness, the security light too far along to shed any light down the grey stone slabs. He hoped the door wasn't locked. He'd never been down there before but was working on the theory that the diner was open twenty-four hours a day, so why bother locking the delivery door? The generator powered the electricity. The boiler supplied the heat. That was transmitted through under-floor heating ducts, and that meant vents in the floor. The boiler room was right under the office.

He went down the stairs slowly, careful not to slip on the fresh snow. The door didn't even have a lock. Grant opened it and was immediately enveloped in humid warmth. He closed the door behind him and followed the dingy bricks-and-mortar passage into the darkness. A single light bulb dangled from the ceiling. The walls were rough and unpainted. There was a door on the left marked fuel store and a set of worn stone steps at the far end with an arrow painted on the brickwork pointing up. Probably some contractor taking the piss. It was obvious that the stairs went up. The door Grant was looking for was on his right. He didn't need to read the Boiler Room sign on the door as he pushed it open.

The boiler room was even darker than the corridor. A dull red bulb in a wire cage on the wall painted the cell in shades of blood. The heat was even more intense, and it felt like Grant had wandered into hell. If that was the case, it was a more pleasant hell than the ones he'd served in overseas. He glanced up at the heavy wooden joists that supported the floor above and felt a twinge of unease. Something didn't add up. He replayed what he'd just heard for clues and came up with the answer straightaway.

Combination lock. Only a small thing. Buried into the concrete.

Mickey Frevert, suffering from a case of verbal diarrhoea. Also suffering from a case of exaggeration. Because the office floor wasn't concrete. It was wooden joists and heavy-duty floorboards. Grant was about to condemn Frevert as a liar when he remembered a post office burglary he'd attended once on Ravenscliffe. A sub–post office in a newsagents shop, not a fully alarmed main office. The burglars had broken into the cellar and gone for the safe. They didn't even have to enter the securely grilled and alarmed shop because the safe was a floor safe and the floor was wooden joists and floorboards. The safe had been sunk into a block of concrete, but the concrete was bolted between two joists. The burglars had spent all night sawing through the wood but ran out of time before the shop opened. The shopkeeper was greeted by a hole in the floor and the safe dangling into the void by the ironwork embedded in the concrete.

Footsteps sounded overhead, and a door banged open.

The office floor creaked under the combined weight of three heavies, a prisoner, and his captor. Grant looked at the uneven block of concrete hanging between the joists like a deadly wasps' nest. Muffled voices sounded from the corner of the room near the safe.

The heating vent.

Grant kept his head bowed beneath the low ceiling and went over to the vent. He closed his eyes and tried to picture the office layout. The door opened inwards from the secondary corridor. The office was small. There was a sturdy wooden desk with a swivel chair to one side and a grey metal filing cabinet against the wall. A window looked out across the rear car park. The telephone Grant had used was on the desk, which was directly above the wasps' nest of concrete that contained the floor safe.

The heating vent was next to the door.

Grant moved his ear to the vent and listened.

There was a rustle of clothing, some more footsteps, then the office fell silent. Somebody coughed. There was a gentle bump on the floor, then a tearing noise. The circle of carpet being ripped from the floor. Somebody tapped the safe with a metallic object. The lead robber spoke directly above Grant's head.

"What's the combination?"

"I don't know. I'm a chef."

Frevert sounded like he'd grown in confidence. Grant remembered Steven Seagal playing an ex-navy SEAL in *Under Siege*. He kept insisting he was just a cook. It would be helpful if Frevert was an ex-navy SEAL, but Grant doubted it. The chef's newfound confidence burst with a slap and a groan.

"How many no-fingered chefs do you know?"

There was a moment's silence while Frevert considered if he should answer.

"None."

Another slap and a groan. Wrong answer.

"Have you ever been to the butchers and got a pork pie? Then, when you bite into it, there's a fingernail or something buried in the gristle? Well, if you don't come over here and open this fucking safe, they'll be finding finger parts in pies for six months."

This time the silence was more intense. Grant could picture Frevert sweating over what to say that wouldn't entail him losing body parts. There was a whimper of indecision. A creak of floorboards as the leader stood up from the safe.

"Think of this like *The Weakest Link*. The answer needs to be correct and banked in time. But you've got to answer or let your fingers do the walking."

A groan sounded overhead. One of the heavies putting the arm on the skinny chef. When Frevert spoke again, Grant could hear the strain in his voice.

"I can't."

"Can't what?"

"Open the safe."

"Not on moral grounds, I hope. Not if you're fond of your fingers."

"No. No. Honest. I don't know the combination. I only work in the kitchen."

The quiet that followed stretched into an awkward silence. Either the leader was preparing to break Frevert's fingers or he was considering whether the chef was telling the truth. The verdict came down on the truth.

"They wouldn't leave the diner open with nobody able to get in the safe. Cough up or say goodbye to this little piggy."

Frevert sounded confused.

"Thought the little piggy rhyme was toes."

"Fingers. Toes. I'll chop your whole fuckin' arm off in a minute."

Fear choked Frevert's apology but not his explanation.

"Wendy. Wendy's got the combination."

"Who the fuck's Wendy?"

GRANT DIDN'T WAIT TO hear the answer. He had maybe thirty seconds before the heavies came out of the office to search for the missing waitress. He wanted to be up the stairs and out of the rear hallway before that happened. He laid the mental floor plan of the office over the cellar layout as he turned right along the dingy passage. The stairs at the end must come out in that corridor. The boiler room was directly under the office. That meant the landing door was a good twelve feet farther along. He took the steps two at a time and stopped with his fist around the handle.

He opened the door a crack and listened for movement. Nothing. The opening faced the wrong way to look towards the office. Too bad. He was making a break for it anyway. He opened the door and was sprinting along the corridor before it closed behind him. Into the main corridor and turn left towards the restaurant. The fridge door was on the left now and the pantry on the right.

Part of his mind was wondering why Rivers had denied having a safe to the first robbers, but his main focus was getting her out before the leader could threaten her with digital amputation.

The pantry door didn't creak. He yanked it open and darted inside. The door closed without a thump. Grant dropped to his knees to help Rivers out of the bottom shelf. He moved the boxes to one side and reached a hand for her to grab. She didn't take it. He bowed his head to look into the shadowy space. It was empty. Wendy Rivers had gone.

02:20 HOURS

GRANT DIDN'T HAVE TIME to wonder where she'd gone. First order of business was not to get caught himself. Being cornered in a pantry with only one door was not the way to do that. He quickly scanned the other shelves, then was back out the door in three seconds. That meant the heavies would be coming out of the office any time now and most likely heading this way. They'd no doubt search every room on their way back to the dining area before widening the perimeter.

The corridor was now a one-way street. The flow of traffic was reversed. Grant couldn't go out the back door because that would be heading towards the robbers. He turned right, and three strides saw him back in the restaurant. Somewhere out front, beyond the broad windows, his Ford Mondeo waited for him to make good his escape. Making good his escape without Rivers and Frevert wasn't an option.

Don't go wading in without communication or backup.

He'd already waded in without backup, so communication was the next step. Get in touch, then wait for the cavalry. There was a wall phone behind the counter. He started to pick it up when a door slammed along the corridor.

Not the cavalry. The heavy mob. Grant put the handset back and skirted the end of the counter. The till was still open, but the cash drawer was empty apart from small change. The display shelves were empty, too, the cigarettes waiting on the floor in three cardboard boxes. Whatever else happened, the crooks would be back for their spoils. This wasn't the place to be. The side door near the toilets was at the other end of the restaurant. The front door was nearer. Grant navigated round the tables and went straight out the front.

The door had barely closed behind him before two of the heavies burst out of the corridor. The limper and his partner. The other two were probably searching the storage rooms, including the pantry and the walk-in fridge. Grant didn't wait to find out. Keeping under the shelter of the overhang, he rounded the corner. The snow was still coming straight down. There was no wind. There was a two-feet-wide band of clear ground along the side of the diner. He'd left enough footprints for now. No reason to point the intruders in his direction.

He reached the drainpipe oil drum and glanced inside. The knotted sack with the little fella was still bundled in the bottom. Grant wondered if he had a mobile on him, then looked across at the Transit van. He wasn't going to start untying the midget to search his pockets, but there was half a chance his mobile might be in the van. Grant wasn't much of a mobile phone man, but he'd seen his colleagues slip their phones on the dashboard when on patrol.

The snow had covered Grant's struggle to disable the driver. There was no avoiding leaving fresh prints. He scanned the side of the diner in case he'd missed any windows. He hadn't. The van was only ten feet away. Grant covered the ground quickly and climbed in the driver's side. He shut the door without slamming it and rummaged through the glove compartment, door pockets, and dashboard. There was no phone.

Radios. In all the *Die Hard* films, the villains always had radios. He checked again. No radios. So much for life imitating art, if Bruce Willis calling everyone a motherfucker was art. It had been a long shot. Grant hadn't noticed the robbers using radio communication. The thieves around Bradford thought Radio Shack was an American basketball player.

Grant got out of the van and crossed to the shelter of the roof. The snow was getting heavier. He wondered how long it would be before the Environment Agency closed Snake Pass to traffic. It happened four or five times every winter. The peaks of the A57 were always the worst affected. Along with the M62, it was always the first to close. If that happened, there'd be no passing motorists to beg a call from, and any cavalry charge he managed to arrange would be slowed to a skidding trickle.

He poked his head around the rear corner, then back again. The only movement was the steam pluming around the generator exhaust. It was cold. Even in his creased leather coat and gloves, he was beginning to feel the nip. He wished he were back in the boiler room. At least there the warmth had been positively—

The thought was stillborn. His mind focused on the obvious thing that he'd overlooked. Not the boiler room but the room directly above it. The office. Now that the heavies were looking for Rivers and the combination, the office would be empty. Even if they weren't dragging Frevert around with them, they wouldn't lock him in the office. The manager's telephone was in the office. Grant should know. He'd used it once before.

The overhang continued to provide shelter from the falling snow. Grant kept close to the building line as he passed the fire exit door, then skirted the wire enclosure. He walked through the cloud of steam and came out at the cellar steps. He went down them carefully. The snow was deeper this time. When he entered the passageway, it felt like he was going round in circles.

A muffled bang reverberated through the ceiling. Grant tensed. The vibration stopped almost immediately. A gunshot? An explosion? He didn't think so. He'd experienced both before, and this didn't feel like that. He followed the passage to the internal stairs and paused again. There was another muffled bang, followed swiftly by another. The heavy thud shook dust from the ceiling.

He opened the door a crack. The opening was facing the wrong way. He couldn't look along the corridor towards the office, but he was certain that was where the banging was coming from. He closed the door and leaned against the wall at the top of the stairs. When the next bang came, he closed his eyes and tried to pinpoint its source. He was right. Somebody was hammering in the office, and he didn't think it was Mickey Frevert trying to escape.

The heavies were hedging their bets. They weren't relying solely on finding the combination. They were going the sub–post office route—trying to open the floor safe with brute force and ignorance. Right beneath the desk that held the office telephone.

GRANT SIDLED BACK DOWN the stairs and waited beside the boiler room door. If the robbers had left one man trying to break open the safe, that wasn't too much of a problem. They weren't tooled up with shooters, just baseball bats and muscle. Grant might have been a typist in the military, but the army taught everyone unarmed combat before any specialist training. One man wasn't the problem; disabling that one man before he could shout for help was. Four against one wasn't good odds. Grant wasn't a one-man fighting machine. He wasn't Jack Reacher or James Bond. He was a West Yorkshire copper with a few extra skills.

He'd been right. He had come full circle. He'd been round the front of the diner. He'd been round the back of the diner. He'd been in the restaurant and the pantry and the boiler room. He'd even been on the roof. None of it had brought him any closer to—

For the second time in five minutes, the thought was stillborn. Something he had seen came back to him. When he was on the roof sneaking up on the getaway driver, a brief glimmer of light had reflected in the darkness—not from the neon sign on the rooftop but up on the hillside behind it. The owner's house that had been standing empty for the last couple of years. Empty but not derelict. It was part of the package that came with leasing the roadside café. Nobody lived there, but that didn't mean the utilities had been turned off. It didn't mean the telephone had been disconnected either.

02:35 HOURS

THE HOUSE STOOD ON the brow of a hill behind the truck stop. A sweeping gravel road curled round the hill from the car park and disappeared beyond a tree-lined ridge that sheltered one side of the building. It was the top floor and gable end that Grant had seen from the diner roof, the neon sign reflecting in the bedroom windows. The rest of the house was just a block of darkness in the greater dark, dusted with white as the snowfall became heavier.

Grant went back along the underground passage to the rear door. Somewhere inside the diner complex, Wendy Rivers was frightened and hurt, hiding in a corner or a secret place that Grant didn't have time to look for. Bumping into the search party would do neither of them or Mickey Frevert any good. Grant needed to call for backup, and he needed to do it now.

The steps leading up from the boiler room exit were an inch deep in snow. The flakes drifting out of the sky were big and fluffy and settling. Wherever he went now, he'd be leaving a trail of foot-prints. The upside was that those footprints would fill in quickly. Even so, the road up to the house was too exposed.

Grant stuck his head above the top of the stairwell and looked around. The search party hadn't extended to the outside yet. He climbed the steps and jogged across the car park to the opposite end of the hill from the road. The incline was gentle but rose steeply behind the industrial wheelie bins in the far corner. He used the bins as a starting point and began to climb.

Ten feet up the hill and the silence sucked in around him. The pine trees lining the ridge and the falling snow absorbed any sounds coming from the diner. Even the rhythmic hammering from the office was muffled to a whisper. The farther up the hill Grant climbed, the quieter it became. Soon the only sound was the beat of his heart and the rasp of his breath.

At first, from the lower reaches of the hillside, the house disappeared, but soon the gable end stood out from the ridgeline, then the bedroom windows, followed by the porch roof and the ground-floor extension. Grant's eyes adjusted to the dark. The snow helped. The ground was white and getting deeper. He was surprised he hadn't seen a gritter truck salting the A57.

The leather coat kept the snow out but not the cold. He pulled the collar up around his neck and thumped his gloved hands together. Snow settled in his hair and steam bloomed around his head as his breathing grew heavier. By the time the hill began to level out, he could see the entire house. He paused beside the trunk of a twisted pine and let his military training kick in. Never approach an enemy position until you've examined all the possible threats. The house might not be occupied, but the principle still applied. It was ingrained in him.

The house was a detached two-story brick building with peaked roofs but no dormer windows in the sloping sides. There were traditional windows on the upper floor and a flat roofed extension to one side. A wooden porch with a slate roof covered the front door. The curtains were closed on all the windows and there were no lights inside. The only movement was the falling snow. As far as he could tell there were no footprints leading to the front door or around the side of the house. Nobody home. Nobody visiting. No threats.

Grant crossed the uneven ground to the house. The fresh snow crunched under his feet, more of a muffled groan than a crunching sound. His ears had become so attuned to the quiet that he could hear dripping water from a broken drainpipe above the flat-roofed extension. He stopped and listened. There was no other noise. The silence was complete. He scanned the facing walls for alarm sensors and security lights. He didn't want to trigger a blinding light when he approached the house. There were none. He doubted if the owners had gone to the expense of alarming an empty property with nothing to steal. The diner was their main source of income, and that was manned twenty-four hours a day.

He changed his mindset from that of a policeman to a burglar. He'd done it often enough when giving crime prevention advice. Now he was going to put it into practice. What would be the easiest point of entry? Like most overnight burglars, the first choice would be an unlocked door, so Grant walked to the porch and tried the door handle.

Locked but worth a try. Next he went to the patio doors built into the end of the extension. It wasn't the traditional conservatory but he could see through a gap in the curtains that it contained wicker furniture and dried grasses. The patio doors were locked. So much for the easy options. Grant turned his attention to the ground floor windows. They were all closed. The upstairs windows too.

Nobody had been sloppy and left any open. It looked like Grant was going to have to force entry as quietly as possible.

He started at the porch and worked his way round the building. The windows were old-fashioned wooden framed and single glazed, but they weren't rotting and they weren't loose. The simplest thing would be to break a window and release the catch, but even in muffled silence the noise would carry. He didn't want to alert the heavies that he was up here. Taking his cue from the ancient windows, he considered how else the structure had dated. The weak spot in most houses was the place where the owners spent the least money. Kitchen windows were frequently overlooked, but the room that was most often neglected was the smallest room in the house: the downstairs toilet.

Coming round the back of the house, Grant found what he wanted plus something he did not. The ground floor toilet window was even older than the other frames and used the outdated glazing of yesteryear. Louvered windows. Four slats of glass fitted horizontally into tilting aluminium frames that could be opened in unison to let air in but not the cat out. Grant had attended plenty of burglaries where the intruders had bent the tip of the aluminium and removed two or three louver slats. Easy peasy lemon squeezy.

That was the good part.

The bad part was that the downstairs toilet was over a double-wide basement garage entrance with a sloping concrete drive for easy access. The ramp was crisscrossed with tire tracks that were rapidly filling with snow.

02:45 HOURS

Grant stared at the tire tracks but couldn't tell how old they were. Definitely after the snow had started, but they were already completely filled with fresh snow. He also couldn't tell if they were coming in or going out. Footprints in the snow could give you a pointer, facing this way or that, but tire tracks were the same whichever way they went.

He listened.

There was no sound of engines and no noises from inside the house. Maybe somebody was using the garage for undercover parking or the diner used it for extra storage. Either way, there didn't seem to be anybody in the garage now, so maybe the tracks were going away. Grant had no control over that.

He concentrated on what he did have control of. The louver windows and the telephone. He tested the strength of the aluminium struts. As usual, they were soft and flimsy. He prised up the bottom of the left-hand strut and then the corresponding strut on the right. The lower pane of glass slid out into his hands. He leaned it against the wall.

Five minutes later and three other panes joined the first. He poked his head through the gap and listened again. Silence inside the house. He checked the room for obstacles. It was a standard downstairs toilet suite with a matching pedestal washbasin next to the toilet. The low-mounted cistern was just below the windowsill. The toilet lid was down. Grant hoisted himself up over the sill, but there wasn't enough room to swing his legs through the opening. He folded at the waist and went in headfirst, resting his hands on the toilet lid until he could bend his legs. He looked like a broken crab but at least he was inside.

Once he was standing upright, he listened again. The wall of silence outside was different than in here. Snow and fir trees muffled the sounds of the night. Inside the darkened house, the quiet was harsher, highlighting every little move he made. The floor creaked. His watch clicked against the washbasin and echoed in the tiled room, but it was still basically silent.

He opened the door into the hallway and waited for his eyes to adjust from the shifting dark outside to the motionless dark in the house. Slowly shapes became visible. Squares of lighter dark showed where the windows were. An angled slope picked out the staircase and banister rail leading upstairs. A tall, rectangular block of darkness in front of him was a door into another room. Grant opened it and was surprised to discover that the kitchen was fully furnished. A dining table and chairs. A toaster and kettle on the worktop. The gentle hum of a refrigerator in the corner. Not exactly an empty house.

He opened a door in the far wall and entered the living room. This too had furniture and household items neatly arranged in the large square room. A television in the corner. A recorder underneath it with a blinking digital clock. A fold-down dining table with two chairs under the front window. Light from the truck stop sign made it brighter in here.

Enough to see the cigarette butts in the ashtray on the table.

Grant stood still in the middle of the room. There was suddenly the very real possibility that he'd just broken into an occupied dwelling. An innocent family could be sleeping upstairs right now. He glanced at the ceiling and blocked out the gentle hum of the fridge as he tried to pick out any sounds from upstairs. Snoring or breathing or the restless movement of the not quite asleep.

There was nothing.

He crossed to the table and held one hand over the cigarette butts. They were cold. Then he ran his finger over the table like his sergeant major on inspection day. His sergeant major would have been apoplectic. The table was thick with dust. Grant did the same with the TV. Dusty. And the mantelpiece. Even worse. He went to the settee and slapped a cushion. A cloud of dust exploded into the gloom. The house might be furnished, but it definitely wasn't occupied.

He parted the front curtains and looked outside. He couldn't see the neon sign, but its light feathered the hillside and fringed the tree line. Falling snow became a red and orange cloud in the distance. The light filtered into the living room and made Grant's search that much easier. He looked around the room for the telephone. Most homes these days had one in the lounge. This wasn't most homes. It was a throwback to bygone days when the family dined together and watched TV together and probably did jigsaw puzzles at the fold-down table.

There was no telephone.

Grant ignored the kitchen and opened the only other door. It led back into the hallway. The staircase ran up the far wall. The front door to the porch was on his left and the downstairs toilet door on his right at the back of the house. Out of curiosity, he tried the front door. It was locked. There were no keys in the lock and none hanging on the three brass hooks beside the door.

Good. That reinforced the empty house theory.

His eyes had adjusted sufficiently to see fairly clearly. Wood panelling boxed in the staircase. A door in the panelling led to understair storage; probably the electric meter. Beside the door was a dark wood table with a built-in chair. A shelf under the table held a Yellow Pages and a local telephone directory. The telephone was plugged into the wall. It was the old style curly-wired handset and base unit.

Grant sat in the telephone seat and picked up the handset. He held it to his ear and sent out a little prayer. Not silence. Not disconnected. Please. He waited. His heartbeat sounded loud in his ears. The brief pause from picking up the phone and holding it to his ear felt like a lifetime. He listened. Silence. Then there was the familiar click of the handset being connected, followed by the dial tone. The phone worked.

Time to call the cavalry.

His fingers hovered over the keyboard. He almost expected it to be the ancient dial type, but it was more modern than that. He tapped the nine, then nine again, then pressed the disconnect button. Dialling 999 would get him the emergency operator. Some call center in god knows where. He'd once been sent to an immediate call in Ecclesfield, an ongoing domestic with a man threatening his wife with a knife. The operator who'd taken the call in Glasgow had got the wrong town and directed Grant to a children's party in the back garden.

He didn't want to wade through the normal questions.

"What emergency service do you require?"

"What is the nature of your emergency?"

"What is your name?"

"Where are you calling from?"

He wanted immediate action and a swift response. He knew the best place to get that. He released the disconnect button and dialed the patrol sergeants' office at Ecclesfield Police Station. Ecclesfield wasn't the covering division, but it was the quickest way to get the message out.

The phone on the other end rang.

Grant let out a sigh of relief.

It continued to ring.

Grant grew impatient. He checked his watch. Almost ten to three in the morning. He hoped the sergeant wasn't in the canteen having a late meal. He hoped the shit hadn't hit the fan on Ravenscliffe and the sergeant was out cleaning up the mess.

It continued to ring.

Grant began to drum his fingers on the table as if that would speed things along. The drumming slowed to the rhythm of his heartbeat. It matched the pulse that was sounding in his ears. It kept time with the *brrr, brrr* of the ringing telephone. The ringing clicked off as the phone was answered.

"Sergeant Ballhaus. Ecclesfield Police Station."

Grant felt a wave of affection for his shift sergeant and was about to speak when the hallway lights came on. Voices sounded from behind the wood panelling, and footsteps began to come up the stairs from the cellar.

02:50 HOURS

GRANT DIDN'T HAVE TIME to speak. He hung up the phone and glanced around the hallway. Living room or kitchen? Neither would give him much opportunity to get out. The front door was locked and the windows were closed. The voices behind the wood panelling grew louder; the footsteps, closer. The patio extension was the only other choice on the ground floor, but even the patio doors were locked. Scrambling out of the toilet window was too risky.

The vibrations from the footsteps were right behind him now.

The voices were foreign.

That was as much as Grant could discern before walking swiftly along the hallway and up the stairs. The steps were carpeted, his footfalls soft, using only the balls of his feet. He reached the first-floor landing and ducked around the banister rail just as the cellar door opened.

"And they think they can get away with this?"

A guttural voice, heavily accented. Eastern European, Grant guessed.

"Who the fuck do they think we are?"

Grant shuffled to the front of the landing and crouched behind the banister. There were four doors. Two were close together at the top of the stairs, the bathroom and small bedroom judging by the nameplates on the doors, not words but cartoons of somebody singing in a bath and somebody else hurling zeds from a bed. The other two doors were at the front of the landing next to Grant. The main bedrooms—one of them directly above the front-porch roof. That would be his preferred exit, but first he listened.

The cellar door slammed shut. Footsteps crossed the hallway into the kitchen, floorboards creaking under the weight. These were big men. Somebody spoke in a foreign language. The first man answered in English.

"Send Bohdan and Marko. Tell them to make it quick."

There was a pause as if the man was making a difficult decision.

"Better finish the cook and the waitress too."

Grant jerked backwards. Who the fuck were these fellas? He knew the influx of East Europeans had changed the country's workforce, but the only ones he'd met were Lithuanians running the hand car wash at Apperley Bridge and the Polish carving out their own little empire in Manningham. Whatever these two were into, it wasn't washing cars.

One set of footsteps came back into the hallway and stopped. "Did somebody leave a window open?"

The second man joined him. "They were told not to."

"They were told not to smoke either, but the ashtray is full again."

The second man sounded confused. "They cannot smoke downstairs."

In the cellar, Grant reckoned he meant.

"Then they had better quit smoking. This house is supposed to be empty. It should not be used as a smoking corner."

Grant pictured Inspector Carr having an illicit cigarette in the designated no smoking zone that was Ecclesfield Police Station. Even the enclosed yard next to the dog kennels. These fellas had obviously instigated their own no smoking zone. The main man spoke again.

"Where is that cold coming from?"

Doors opened and closed as the men checked the kitchen and the living room. The last door to be opened was the downstairs toilet. Grant felt the whoosh of cold air when it was yanked open.

"Has he been smoking through the fucking window?"

A pause before the reply.

"The glass is outside."

Grant didn't wait for the next line. He was already opening the front bedroom door when the first man lowered his voice.

"We have an intruder."

THE BEDROOM DOOR CLOSED without a sound. The room was dark, the only light coming through the tinted window above the door. Grant's eyes were already adjusted to the gloom by the time he turned to scan the bedroom. It was big. A double bed against one wall. Built-in wardrobes along another. A narrow door into the en suite bathroom. A dumbwaiter hatch in the wall. A dressing table next to the door. He considered dragging it across the entrance but decided stealth and secrecy would work better than brute force and ignorance. Hide and be quiet.

Then climb out of the window.

He listened at the door. Footsteps sounded on the stairs. Heavier than Grant's. This fella wasn't trying to be quiet. He probably didn't expect to find an intruder. The louver windows could have been removed at any time. The snow would have already begun to cover them, disguising the timescale.

The footsteps stopped. The bathroom door was flung open so hard, it banged against the wall. He might not be expecting to find an intruder, but he wasn't taking any chances. The rear bedroom door opened next. The footsteps disappeared as the man searched that room. Grant didn't wait for him to come along the landing. He grabbed a pillow from the bed and crossed to the en suite bathroom. After a quick glance inside, he left the door open and went to the window.

The slate roof of the front porch was just a few feet below the sill. Grant checked the frame. The window was an old-fashioned sash type with a screw fastener at the bottom. The screw lock was old and broken, but he hoped the window hadn't been painted shut. It hadn't, but it was stiff from the lack of recent use. He used both hands and a lot of upper body strength to slide it up. It stuck after a couple of inches. He bent his legs to get more weight behind the lift, and it creaked open all the way. The curtains fluttered.

The rear bedroom door slammed shut and the footsteps came along the landing. Grant held his breath. The first door would be the other bedroom if the man was taking them in order. The footsteps came closer. Along the banister rail towards the front of the house. They stopped. Grant ducked his upper body through the window. Then the door opened to the other bedroom. Grant ducked back inside and scanned the room one last time as he listened to the next-door room being searched. He laid the pillow on the edge of the windowsill and gauged the drop.

The East European was big and ugly. His chin was as square as Desperate Dan's and twice as bristly. This fella could shave in the morning and have a five o'clock shadow by noon. He flung the last door on the landing open and entered the front bedroom. The vicious movement of the door wafted the curtains and cool air came in through the open window.

Obvious point of exit.

He crossed to the window and flicked the curtains aside, then stopped. A thought appeared to cross his mind. His brow furrowed. His eyes scanned the room. A narrow door stood partly open. The en suite bathroom. Ignoring the open window, he threw the door open but didn't turn the light on. He'd been ordered to maintain a blackout. It didn't matter. There was nowhere to hide in the bathroom. He let out a gruff bark, then turned back to the window.

The distraction hadn't worked. Open the window but hide in the room. He ducked his head through the opening and looked down. A strip of snow had been knocked off the porch roof. It was already beginning to fill in, making it difficult to work out the time. It didn't matter.

He ducked back into the room and crossed to the landing. Leaning over the banister, he called down to his colleague.

"Gone out the window."

A voice from downstairs. "How long ago?"

"Hard to tell. Snow's filling it in."

There was a pause before the next instruction from downstairs. "Come on, then. Let's get Bohdan and Marko moving."

The bedroom door closed and the footsteps crossed the landing and started down the stairs. Grant slid out from under the bed and listened at the door. The big fella reached the bottom of the stairs and joined his boss. Words were exchanged. The first man raised his voice.

"I said no windows open. Go close it."

There was a murmur of dissent but then the footsteps began to climb the stairs.

Grant darted to the window and swung his leg over the sill. The pillow lay on the ground where he'd slid it down the roof to disturb the snow. At least this time the fella was unlikely to check outside. Grant swung his other leg out onto the porch roof and glanced across the ridgeline towards the diner. He froze with his leg half out of the window.

Wendy Rivers was crouching behind the fenced compound next to the exhaust vent. Steam obscured her upper body but didn't hide the man coming round the side of the building past the fire exit door. As if that wasn't bad enough, headlights swept into the car park from the main road. It stopped beside Grant's Mondeo and the engine clicked off.

Grant recognized the dents in the front bumper. Jamie Hope had obviously got off duty early.

03:00 HOURS

THE GENERAL RULE OF thumb in combat is never split your forces. Grant was in the reverse position in that there were two people to warn and only one of himself. He couldn't split his forces. He had to make a decision on who to protect first. Always back your colleagues was a dyed-in-the-wool credo for all ex-military, but women and children first was ingrained even deeper.

The footsteps behind him reached the landing.

They started towards the bedroom door.

Evade and destroy. That was something else Grant had been trained to do. The first part of that was to get the fuck off the roof. He set both feet on the ridge tiles of the porch and checked for any protrusions on the sloping roof. The last thing he needed was to split his legs open sliding to the ground. There was nothing obvious. There was no guttering along the bottom. There was no time to worry about it. He followed the track of the pillow and let himself go.

The bedroom door opened.

Grant hit the ground in a puff of snow.

The trees were only six feet from the porch. Grant was moving before the shock settled into his knees. Diagonally across the snow and under the shelter of the low branches. Snow and pine needles immediately sucked all the sound out of the night. He crouched beside the nearest tree trunk and listened for the warning yell from the window. The only noise that came was the sash being slammed down. He glanced up at the bedroom. The curtains were still swaying but the window was closed. There was no face looking down. Grant was clear.

Car park or rear compound?

There was only one clear choice. Hope would have a bit more time before he got out of the car and crossed the car park to the diner. Rivers was in more immediate danger. Grant dodged through the trees and came back out on the slope he'd climbed twenty minutes ago. Keeping his breathing controlled and his footsteps quiet, he kept his eyes on Rivers all the way down the hillside.

Steam from the exhaust took some of the chill off, but Wendy Rivers couldn't help shivering. Part of it was the cold but the rest was shock and panic at being hit in the face twice, with the threat of worse to come. She rubbed her hands together, then wrapped both arms tight around her chest. It didn't warm her in the slightest. She was cold and miserable and sick of getting snowed on.

Somebody coughed farther along the building line—near the fire exit door just beyond the compound. She held her breath and listened. Shambling footsteps coming towards her in the snow. She shuffled backwards out of the steam and turned away from the sound.

There was a sudden flurry of activity, then silence.

She stood still, half crouched in the shadows. All she could hear was her own breathing loud in her ears. Two choices. Follow the filled-in tracks towards the wheelie bins or clamber down the steps to the boiler room corridor. Her mind wrestled with the dilemma. One course of action would leave her exposed as she crossed the open ground, and the other would have her cornered in the cellar.

She took a deep breath and made her decision. Her thighs forced her upright and she was about to sprint across the rear car park when a hand clamped over her mouth and strong arms dragged her backwards.

Grant kept his hand clamped tight until Rivers stopped struggling. Her eyes went from wild panic to angry recognition, then gentle resignation. She glanced behind Grant at the crumpled figure on the ground. Grant made soothing noises until he reckoned she was calm enough to release.

He took his hand from her mouth.

She gave a violent shake of the head and flexed her lips. "This isn't my idea of you being the hero."

"It isn't my idea of being off-duty either. Hang on a minute."

He went over to the inert figure and unfastened the heavy's belt. He pulled it out, then sat the man up against the fence. Threading the leather through the wire links, he looped it around the muscle-bound neck and yanked it tight. Just too high for comfort. Not high enough to strangle him. He unzipped the man's coat halfway, then tugged it off his shoulders, pinning his arms at his sides so he couldn't reach the belt when he woke up. A quick search of his pockets for other weapons, then Grant picked the baseball bat up out of the snow and went back to Rivers.

"Let's get you out of the cold."

He wrapped one arm around her shoulders and guided her towards the cellar steps. His footprints from before were completely filled with fresh snow. He threw a quick glance skyward. The flakes were as big as butterflies now. It was only a matter of time before Snake Pass was closed. Getting away before the snow got too deep was the priority now.

The cellar passage brought welcome respite from the cold. Grant's other priority was Jamie Hope. He would be walking into the middle of an armed robbery any minute now. Grant tried to send a psychic message reminding the probationer what he'd told him earlier. *Doesn't give you shit-all in a pub fight with no baton and stab vest.* Referring to his police warrant card. He didn't want Hope steaming in, off-duty and without communication or backup, and ordering the heavies to cease and desist.

There was a tactical advantage to be gained here, though. Grant shepherded Rivers into the boiler room and listened for the hammering upstairs. The big fella trying to force the safe open. The office was quiet. Headlights sweeping across the car park had provided a fortuitous distraction. Jamie Hope's arrival had drawn their attention and left the safe unguarded. Grant kept his tone friendly as he looked into Rivers's eyes.

"I thought you told 'em there wasn't a safe."

"I thought you said you were off-duty."

"Funny thing about duty times. If you have an accident on the way home from work, you're still classed as being on-duty. So you can claim compensation as an injury on-duty."

"This is classed as an accident?"

"I didn't stumble into the robbery on purpose."

“Me neither.”

“But you did tell ’em there was no safe.”

“First reaction.”

“Master chef said there was no money in the safe.”

“There isn’t.”

“So what’s in there that’s worth robbing the diner for?”

“I have no idea.”

The boiler pulsed heat into the cellar. It throbbed as the pressure pumped warm air around the under-floor heating ducts. The red bulb in its cage made the room seem even hotter. Grant felt sweat break out on his brow. He took Rivers’s hands in his and gave them a gentle squeeze.

“Master chef said you know the combination.”

“That’s right.”

“So why don’t we go find out?”

03:10 HOURS

THE SECONDARY CORRIDOR WAS clear as they came out from the service stairs. Grant could hear raised voices coming from the dining area but no sounds of violence. He felt a twinge of guilt at leaving Hope to his own devices for the moment but was calmed by the knowledge that although this was an armed robbery, the heavies were using baseball bats instead of guns. An off-duty policeman would initially get harsh words and threats instead of having his brains bashed in. Grant already had a plan for separating Hope from the robbers.

First order of business was the safe.

He paused to confirm that the hammering noise from the office had stopped, then led Rivers along the corridor. The office door was open. The room was empty. But it wasn't tidy. Grant had to give them points for effort. Whoever had been given the job of opening the safe had unleashed hell on the gleaming circle of metal in the floor. Not on the safe door itself but the surrounding enclosure. Unlike the post office burglary, the man hadn't tried to cut the floor joists, preferring the hammer and chisel approach. Chunks of concrete had been chipped away, forming a deep channel around the safe door. He hoped the hammering hadn't damaged the lock, but he supposed instructions had been given to chisel the safe out of the floor rather than destroy the combination dial. They were still working on plan A. Find the waitress and get her to open the safe.

The waitress was standing next to Grant. He closed the door behind them but left a half-inch gap so he could hear if the main restaurant door opened. Rivers took a deep breath. Grant stepped aside and made a gentlemanly "ladies first" gesture. She didn't need asking twice.

Rivers cleared a patch of carpet and knelt beside the safe. The circle of carpet had been removed and the desk upended against the wall. The filing cabinet had been pushed into that corner too, making the office look as if it had been tilted on the *Titanic*, all the furniture sliding to one end. Grant dropped to one knee to watch.

She flexed her fingers and wiggled them in the air.

Grant couldn't hide his impatience.

"Come on. You're not safecracking. You know the combination."

"If I was safecracking, I'd have a stethoscope."

Grant ignored the sudden chill that image provoked.

"So what's with the finger-wiggling thing?"

"It helps me remember."

He raised his hands in surrender.

"Sorry. Go for it."

She took a deep breath, then let it out slowly through her mouth. She closed her eyes for a moment, and when she opened them again she was completely focused. Using her left hand for balance as she leaned forward, the fingers of her right hand settled on the dial. She gave it an extended twist in both directions to clear the numbers, then zeroed the dial.

Her lips intoned the numbers as her fingers worked the dial.

"Seventeen right."

The dial settled on seventeen, right.

"Thirty-two left."

In one sweeping movement, the dial spun past zero to thirty-two, left.

"And forty-seven right."

She performed the final twist of the dial, then turned the handle.

Nothing happened.

"Shit."

Grant leaned forward. "What? They changed the combination?"

Rivers sat back on her haunches. "No. I always get it wrong the first time."

She began to hum the theme from *The Bridge on the River Kwai.*

Grant sounded exasperated. "This isn't the time for relaxation exercises."

Rivers stopped humming and glared at him. "This is the perfect time for relaxation exercises. But that's not what I'm doing. It's the Colonel Bogey march."

Grant looked blank.

Rivers smiled.

"To remind me. When you're marching, you always start with left, right, left. I did it the wrong way."

She leaned forward and reset the dial. Following the same routine she entered the correct combination. Seventeen left. Thirty-two right. Forty-seven left. Left, right, left. She turned the handle.

A loud click filled the office.

The heavy disc of the safe door came up in her hand, and she laid it on the floor. They both leaned forward to look inside. Mickey

Frevert had been right. There was no money in the safe. There wasn't much of anything except a large brown envelope curled around the inside so it would fit. Grant looked at Rivers and raised his eyebrows. She shrugged her shoulders. Grant reached in and pulled the envelope out. It felt thick and sturdy. He already knew what the contents were before he slit the flap and took them out.

A dozen black-and-white surveillance photographs. The first two or three were fairly innocuous shots of a man and a woman entering a seedy hotel. Grant could tell it was seedy because there was rubbish in the entrance and a wino glugging from a bottle beside the door. The rest of the pictures didn't waste any more time with establishing shots; they cut right to the chase. Oral sex. Anal sex. Ride-'em-cowboy sex. And splatter-it-all-over-your-face cum-shots. The woman's face wasn't familiar even before it was redecorated. The man's face had been all over the news recently arguing for stricter controls on imports and exports at sea and air terminals across the north.

The door banged open.

"A local councillor is a good man to have on your side."

The leading robber wasn't alone. Jamie Hope was clamped across the mouth by one of the heavies, and Mickey Frevert looked as if he'd lost the will to live. Hope and Frevert were dwarfed by the towering bulk of the robbers, but it wasn't size that mattered tonight. The baseball bats had been replaced by nasty-looking skinning knives. Even with one robber tied to the compound fence and the midget dumped in a barrel, the odds were still in the villains' favor. It was the knives that tipped the balance, despite the kitchen knife down the back of Grant's trousers.

The main man held out a hand.

“I’ll take those, thank you.”

The air sucked out of Grant’s lungs as he realized his mistake. He glanced at the overturned desk and the clutter of office equipment and stationery dumped on the floor behind it. A curly wire and offensive green handset lay among the ruins. The base unit was still plugged into the wall socket. The dialing tone had long since timed out, but the telephone was still in good working order. That should have been Grant’s first order of business while Rivers opened the safe. *Don’t go charging in waving your warrant card without communication or backup.*

Grant had been kneeling next to the means of calling for backup and had completely ignored it. He pushed up from the crouch and straightened his back. His knees cracked like gunshots in the silence. The leader waved his hand for Grant to pass him the photos. Grant slid them into the envelope and closed the flap. He tapped the envelope twice while he calculated time and distance. Not the distance between him and the nearest robber or the time it would take to drive an elbow into his throat but the time it would take Bohdan and Marko to cover the distance from the house on the hill.

03:20 HOURS

"Give it to me."

The friendliness went out of the robber's voice.

Grant kept his response light and chatty as he handed the envelope over.

"You should be careful what you ask for. It might be exactly what you get."

The leader ignored the threat as he looked at Hope's uniform trousers and then at Grant's. He reached over and opened the top of Grant's leather coat. Neither of the late-shift policemen had changed into civvies when going off-duty, preferring the normal routine of traveling in half-and-half—civilian coats over their uniform shirt and trousers.

"Off-duty coppers. Who'd have guessed?"

Grant shrugged but kept quiet. Hope took the hint from his tutor. Frevert groaned as he dabbed blood from his swollen face. Rivers looked frightened as she glanced nervously at the wall clock. Grant tried to lighten the mood.

"Isn't this where you tell the prisoners about your wicked evil plan?"

The leader shook his head. "No wicked evil plan."

He waved the envelope, which was thick with photographs again. "He used to work for them. Now he works for us."

Grant waited for the leader to explain himself. They always did in the pictures. Villains were always telling James Bond about their plans for world domination just before they ordered his death. Then, when he managed to escape, he knew just what to do to stop them. In the pictures. This was real life. In real life, villains kept their mouths shut and gave away as little as possible. All this fella showed was a nod of the head towards the door.

"Cooler."

There was no witty response. Grant knew he wasn't Steve McQueen in *The Great Escape*. They were about to be herded into the walk-in fridge opposite the pantry. Provided he didn't stall the villains any longer, Grant reckoned they could be safely locked away before Bohdan and Marko arrived to take care of these fellas. To finish the chef and the waitress too. *Who the fuck do they think we are?* Grant didn't want to be out in the open when he found out, but he did want to find out. He reassessed his priorities. Main thing now was not to be hanging with the burglars when the East Europeans arrived.

He let out a sigh and slumped his shoulders to indicate surrender, then allowed himself to be led out along the corridor. The pantry would have been better, but the fridge would do. This wasn't a purpose-built truck stop. It had been added to and extended over the years. He would learn more once they were safely locked inside. It would be cold in the refrigerator, but Grant had a feeling things were going to warm up out here.

The refrigerator door was yanked open, and Grant was relieved to see it was only a fridge and not a freezer. What he wasn't happy about was being searched before they were shoved in there. The big fella with the limp wasn't gentle. He took the knife out of Grant's belt and the car keys out of his pocket. A firm push forced Grant inside, then the others were searched too. Hope and Frevert had their phones smashed on the floor. Hope's car keys were taken. The big fella put them in his coat pocket. Grant made a mental note for later. Two cars parked outside meant he could get all four of them to safety with ease—once he got the keys back.

Rivers was the last to get searched. There was nothing to take but plenty to grope. Her curves were examined in detail before she was pushed through the door into the fridge. Anger replaced the clock-watching worry on her face as the door was slammed shut, locking them in. At least the interior light stayed on, this not being your traditional fridge where the light went off when the door closed.

Everybody let out a collective sigh that plumed steam into the air. Nobody spoke for a few minutes. Grant did what he always did when he entered a new location: scanned the room for exits and windows. This being a refrigerator meant there were no windows and only one door, but since this was an afterthought fridge meant he was right about the other thing. He didn't mention it for now. There were other things to discuss first.

"Jamie. What the fuck are you doing here?"

The teenage policeman blushed but squared his shoulders. "Well. It's good to see you too."

For the second time that night, Grant felt bad about being so harsh with his probationer. He nodded and patted Hope on the back. Hope nodded too.

"Thought you could use some company. Sarge let me off early 'cause of the other business, and I knew you'd be here."

Grant let out a sigh. "Thanks. But I'm your tutor. You're my responsibility. That makes one more responsibility than I need right now."

Hope proved why he was a prospect. "You're only responsible for me when we're on-duty. You're off-duty now."

Grant slitted his eyes and stared at Hope. "A copper's never off-duty."

Hope slapped his thigh and grinned. "I knew it. All that stuff about ignoring a crime off-duty being unethical—I knew you'd never ignore a crime."

"Fuck unethical. This isn't a bunch of drunks fighting outside the Chinese and it isn't a junky nicking citric acid. You lot are my responsibility because that's what I do. So shut the fuck up and let me figure out our exit strategy."

Hope deflated in front of Grant's eyes. Grant vowed to work on his anger management skills. He put an arm around Hope's shoulders and gave him a friendly squeeze. "Thanks for coming, though. We're gonna need your help."

That wasn't strictly true. Grant preferred to work alone in situations like this. It was the situation he needed to discuss next.

"Wendy. What goes on up at the house?"

Rivers blinked back to life.

"The house?"

Grant watched her eyes.

"Up the hill round the back."

Her expression fluctuated between frank openness and being caught in a lie. She appeared to decide on openness.

"It's owned by the diner. Live-in accommodation for the manager, but nobody lives there at the moment. I think they lease it out for storage."

"Who to?"

"I don't know. Some foreign guys."

"Like you?"

"Not American. Russians or something. I've heard trucks delivering round back now and then."

"Delivering what?"

She shrugged. "Don't know."

Her eyes were clear and steady. Either she was a very good liar or she really didn't know what was coming in on the trucks. Grant decided to share a bit of extra information.

"Well, I was up there trying to use the phone. Almost bumped into a couple of East Europeans who aren't happy about those fellas out there. They're sending the help to sort 'em out."

Rivers took a deep breath. Hope kept quiet. Mickey Frevert showed he hadn't fully grasped the situation.

"So let 'em. Save us having to sort them out."

Grant considered the diminutive chef who wasn't much taller than the midget he'd bundled into the oil barrel outside. He tilted his head in feigned concentration.

"I don't suppose you're like Steven Seagal in *Under Siege,* are you?"

"What?"

"You know. An ex-navy SEAL who can also cook?"

"I'm just the chef."

"Okay. So when it comes to us sorting them out, what you really mean is the two police officers in the room. Right?"

Frevert looked shamefaced. Grant was two for zero embarrassing folk tonight. He decided to explain how serious this was.

"The two fellas they're sending down to sort this out—they've also been told to finish the chef and the waitress."

Rivers and Frevert gasped in unison. Grant continued.

"I don't think that means handing your notice."

The room fell quiet. Grant let the silence settle into their bones before giving them something else to think about.

"The other question is why would a loss-making diner have blackmail photos in the safe? And how is that connected to the business up at the house?"

Rivers looked blank. The frown of concentration on Frevert's face was almost comical as he took the question seriously. Hope simply waited. He knew a rhetorical question when he heard one. A light went on behind Frevert's eyes.

"The man in the pictures—I've seen him on the news."

Grant threw him an enquiring stare. Frevert gulped. "I saw them in your hand."

True that. Grant had the pictures in full view before slipping them back in the envelope to hand them over. He nodded his approval.

"Me too. Some local councillor campaigning about import/export procedures."

Frevert held his hands out and tilted his head. "That's me tapped out."

Grant was mulling the information over in his head, trying to make the hidden connections. It was all speculation, but he thought he could see the through line.

"Right here—where we are now—we're right in the middle of three airports and two major shipping terminals."

He ticked them off on the fingers of one hand. "Manchester, Leeds/Bradford, and Robin Hood airports."

He waved the hand towards the west. "Liverpool on the west coast."

Then towards the east. "Hull on the east."

He had all their attention now.

"If you were smuggling shit into any of those, having a man of influence in your pocket would be very handy."

Frevert proved he still wasn't up to speed. "Smuggling what?"

Hope proved he was. "What's it always about round here? Drugs. Right?"

Grant nodded his approval. This kid would go far.

"And more than a few dealer bags and rolls of cash under the bath."

The room fell quiet again. Rivers shivered and wrapped her arms around herself. Frevert's teeth began to chatter. For the first time Grant became aware of just how cold it could get in the refrigerator. About the same as being caught outside in a blizzard. He glanced around at the storage shelves. This wasn't an industrial fridge like the one in *The Long Good Friday*, where Bob Hoskins had his gangland rivals brought in upside down on overhead runners. It was a chilled storage room about the size of the pantry across the hall. The same wooden shelving too.

And the same under-floor heating vent.

Except this one was boarded up and disconnected from the boiler.

Grant's exit strategy.

He began to search the shelves. This particular walk-in fridge might well be an afterthought, but one thing all installations had was an emergency toolkit for running repairs. Like having a first-aid kit in a restaurant.

He was checking the second shelf when gunshots exploded outside—a short burst followed by running footsteps. A second burst of gunshots from the other end of the corridor, then silence. Guns. That ramped up the danger. Grant hated guns. Knives were bad enough, but at least they had to get close to use a knife. Guns were an entirely different ballgame.

Footsteps came along the corridor.

They stopped outside the fridge.

The door opened, and a square-jawed man built like a brick shithouse stood in the doorway, a big black gun in one hand. There was blood on the floor. Lots of it. The air smelled of cordite and freshly struck matches. He gestured at the captives with his other hand.

"You. Come here."

He took Rivers by the hand and dragged her out, then shut the door.

03:30 HOURS

MICKEY FREVERT SAT ON the floor and drew his knees up to his chest. He wrapped both arms around his knees and hugged them tight. His teeth were still chattering but not because of the cold. Eyes stared out of a pale face, all the blood having drained at the sound of the gunshots. Jamie Hope knelt down next to him and put a protective arm around his shoulders. Grant was again impressed with the young constable's maturity, but other things needed his attention.

The repair kit.

He continued checking the shelves, concentrating on the first three feet of each shelf from the door. The tools would be within reach of the doorway for easy access. He found the box on the top shelf to the right of the door. It was a small red case just big enough to contain a selection of spanners and screwdrivers, plus a pair of long-nose pliers.

Frevert wasn't for comforting. "You said they were told to finish the chef and the waitress."

Grant paused in his rummaging. "Don't feel left out. They'll have to finish all of us now."

"Why take Wendy first?"

Grant didn't want to think about the possibilities, rape being the obvious first choice. Rivers was the only female. Unless the new threat was into butt fucking, that put her at the top of the list. If the big man was going to kill them all, he could just as easily have shot them from the doorway. So there was something they wanted first, and Grant was afraid he knew what.

"Was she the only one knew the combination?"

"I only worked with Wendy. Could have been others on the day shift."

"Did she ever open the safe?"

"No. She'd have no need to. There wasn't anything in it."

"Well, there was tonight. And I don't see the drugs boys keeping their blackmail photos in the diner safe when they've got the house round back."

"Maybe..." Frevert struggled but in the end was lost for words. "I don't know."

A deep rumbling noise began to shake the room. It reverberated through the ground and rattled the shelves. It grew louder, then faded, only to be replaced by another, then another. A cycle of three. Grant threw an enquiring glance at the chef.

"The boiler?"

Frevert shook his head. "If the pressure was getting too high, it would just keep rumbling."

Grant agreed. It wouldn't rumble, then stop three times. He listened at the door. It was heavy and sealed but not as thick as Grant had first thought. He could hear the dull roar move around the building before it disappeared round the back. Trucks. Big ones. Going up to the house.

"Whatever she heard being delivered. Sounds like it's arriving now."

Hope patted Frevert on the shoulder, then stood up. "Good timing."

Grant looked at his protégé. "Too good to be a coincidence."

Hope pointed at the toolbox. "I don't fancy still being here when they come back for the next one."

Grant nodded, then put the toolbox next to the blocked heating vent. "You ever see *The Great Escape*?"

Hope snorted a laugh. "Only every Christmas."

Grant tapped the vent covering. "We tunnel."

Frevert crawled forward. "Hell yes."

Grant let them select a screwdriver each from the box, then they all set about unfastening the vent. The sound of the trucks faded into the distance. The sound of scraping and prising filled the room.

UNDER-FLOOR HEATING IS AN efficient way of warming your house, but it doesn't need large air ducts to transport the air from room to room—in a normal installation, that is. Whoever had set up the Woodlands Truck Stop and Diner's heating system must have been using leftovers from an industrial-scale project. Like the cowboy builders who'd extended the dining room, it was a botched job.

Grant thanked heaven for small mercies. He slid the vent cover across the floor and stuck his head down the hole. The aluminium panelling was dusty and black. It ran towards the corridor and the restaurant and no doubt forked to cover all the ground floor rooms, including the office. That wasn't the direction Grant wanted to go. He checked the other way. The ventilation duct sloped almost immediately, a gentle incline that was almost as cold as the fridge.

This channel was cut off from the main flow, but there was only one place for it to go. The boiler room.

"It's gonna be a tight squeeze."

He sat against the wall and sized his companions up before settling on Frevert.

"Smallest first. Glad you're not one of those fat lump of lard chefs, always dipping into their own food."

"You haven't tasted my food."

"Actually, I have. Once."

"Just the once?"

"Yes."

"There you go, then. Now you know why I'm night cook for an empty diner."

Grant pointed a finger downward, then towards the boiler room.

"Okay, Mighty Midget. Across, then down. Take the screwdriver with you. You'll have to prise the vent open. Should drop you into the boiler room. Wait for me there."

Frevert nodded, then slid his head and shoulders into the hole. Grant watched him disappear along the channel but his mind changed direction. Mighty Midget? As soon as Grant was out and free, he was going to need some answers. The robbers had no doubt been rounded up or killed. He hoped they'd missed the little fella tied up in the oil barrel.

"Okay, Jamie. You next."

Hope looked at his tutor and nodded towards the hole in the floor.

"Shouldn't you go? Secure the exit and make sure he's okay?"

Grant looked at the teenage probationer who was having to grow up fast.

"Have I done your six-month assessment yet?"

"My progress report?"

"Yes."

"Thought you only did one after the first year."

"That's normally the case. But this isn't normal. If I was to do a six-month report right now, I'd say you were going to make an outstanding police officer and be a credit to the force. So. You can secure the exit and make sure Mickey's okay. All right?"

Hope's chest filled with pride. "Thanks. All right. What about you?"

Grant indicated the fridge door.

"I'm going to make sure our exit is secure and nobody comes after us."

Hope looked excited.

"Booby-trap it? Like in *The A-Team*? Making explosives out of baking powder and stuff?"

"That report just got taken down a notch. No. I'm not going to booby-trap it."

He pointed at the vent cover and kicked a sack of flour. "I'm gonna cover it so nobody sees the vent. Now go."

Hope blushed like the teenager he was, then tapped his forehead. "Gotcha."

He ducked his head and shoulders into the hole and slithered along after Frevert. The air duct popped and creaked and echoed through the system. Grant hoped there was too much going on outside for the gunmen to hear the noise.

He waited for Hope's feet to disappear, then listened at the fridge door. There was some commotion from the restaurant but no raised voices. He went back to the hole in the floor and picked up the vent cover. It was bent out of shape, but that didn't matter. He laid it on the floor and stood the flour sack on it. Holding the edge of the vent between finger and thumb he pulled the sack across the floor like a sled. It was heavy but moved smoothly.

A door slammed along the corridor.

Footsteps came towards the fridge.

Grant was up in a flash. He stood at the hinge side of the door and held the screwdriver tight in one fist. The footsteps came closer. They were labored and slow. Maybe the limping robber. Something scraped along the floor. The footsteps stopped outside the door. Grant relaxed, ready to move quickly once the villain saw the room was empty.

A door handle clicked open—not the fridge door but the pantry opposite. The shuffling footsteps went in and came straight back out again. The door shut with a click, and whoever was out there went back towards the restaurant.

Grant had wasted enough time. The next intrusion might be in the fridge and not the pantry. He slid the makeshift sled to the edge of the air duct, then lowered himself into the hole feet first. He'd need his hands to cover the hole. The duct was narrow and his shoulders were broader than the other two's, but he managed to scrape his way inside. Just. At the last moment, while he still had enough leverage, he pulled the vent cover across the hole, and the weight of the sack held it in place. Exit secured. Using his feet to guide him, he set off to follow the others.

03:40 HOURS

"JESUS AITCH CHRIST. LOOSE joint almost took my nose off at that last bend."

Grant dropped down into the boiler room and dabbed the side of his nose with the back of his hand. A thin line of blood showed against the whiteness of the skin, about the only patch that wasn't black with grime from the narrow funnel. A jutting piece of metal had caught him as he'd clawed his way through the air duct. Now that he was on solid ground, he flexed his neck and shoulders. He couldn't stretch to his full height because of the low roof.

Hope and Frevert stood in the corner next to the boiler. Both had similar scars; Hope on his cheek and Frevert on his forehead.

"It got you too, huh?"

Hope nodded. Frevert was still in denial. Grant indicated the smaller vent into the office.

"Heard anything from up there?"

Hope shook his head.

"All quiet. Is that the back office?"

"Yes."

Grant looked at the concrete block that cocooned the floor safe. It was still substantial but was leaning to one side on its fastenings. The chiselling and the hammering had splintered the joists but was a long way short of releasing the beehive of uneven concrete. They'd have been at it all night if Grant hadn't got Rivers to open it. Not his greatest moment.

Thinking of Rivers prompted him to get a move on.

"It won't be quiet for long."

He opened the door to confirm that the other room along the passageway was the fuel store, then he examined the system of pipes and valves that controlled the boiler. The pressure gauge was big and round and far too impressive for a back road truck stop. It confirmed what he'd guessed earlier. The owners had cobbled together the refurbishment from anywhere and everywhere. Industrial waste put to good use. The epitome of recycling.

Grant paused to get the plan straight in his mind, then gathered his forces together in a conspiratorial huddle.

"This is what I'm gonna need you to do."

Ten minutes later, the cellar smelled of spilled petrol and oily rags. The red light emphasized the heat from the boiler. The enclosed space strengthened the almost overpowering stench. Grant was beginning to feel lightheaded. He was certain the others were feeling the same.

"Once I go out, wait in the passage if it gets too strong."

Talking made it worse. The gulps of air between sentences.

Grant held a handkerchief over his mouth and nostrils. It was like dealing with a sudden death where the body had become ripe. Handkerchiefs and perfume were the best deterrent. Polo mints and a stiff drink was the perfect antidote. The best they could come up with tonight was a handkerchief or, in the case of Frevert, the sleeve of his chef's smock.

Three petrol cans stood around the base of the boiler. Some had slopped onto the floor when Grant had filled the empty beer bottle he'd found in a crate near the back steps. Empties awaiting collection. The Molotov cocktail was improvised but effective. The fuse was a torn strip of his uniform shirttail. The Zippo lighter had come from Frevert, a heavy smoker whenever he could get out of the kitchen. Car keys and mobile phones had been taken when they were searched, but his cigarettes and lighter had been left in a rare show of compassion.

Grant looked at the five-gallon petrol cans on the bare concrete floor. Big green jerry cans from the army surplus store. He prised the cantilever lids open, then hefted one of the cans in both hands. He poured petrol over the other two cans and splashed it around the boiler before standing the half-empty can next to the other cans.

Hope stepped back towards the door. Frevert stood in front of the pressure gauge with one hand on the valve. Grant waved him away.

"Not until you hear the signal. Remember?"

Frevert looked nervous. Grant wondered if the chef was up to this. He decided he wasn't anything like Steven Seagal's ex-navy SEAL that could also cook, but the options were limited. He'd rather trust Frevert with the pressure valve than rely on him making the call. The chef's voice trembled.

"The signal?"

Grant held up the petrol bomb.

"When the van goes up."

Frevert nodded.

"Got it."

Grant turned to Hope and jerked a thumb at the ceiling.

"The phone's on the floor behind the desk. You know the number?"

"Yes."

"If there's no reply at the patrol sergeants' office, ring the front desk. Just make sure you get through to Sergeant Ballhaus. He'll do the rest."

"Okay."

Grant put a calming hand on Frevert's shoulder.

"How long before the pressure goes critical?"

The chef seemed glad to be asked something he knew the answer to. "Last time they forgot to open the relief valve, it took fifteen minutes before the whole place started shaking. So, maybe twenty minutes, tops."

Worry furrowed his brow as he thought of the consequences.

"There's a lot of pressure in that old thing. It's gonna go with a bang."

Grant smiled a hard little smile. "That's the idea."

He glanced at Hope.

"And Jamie—once you get Ballhaus on the phone, keep it brief. We don't want you being sent into orbit with the safe and the office desk."

Hope smiled back. His smile was full of giddy enthusiasm. "Now we're doing *The A-Team* thing, aren't we?"

"You're too young to remember George Peppard and Mr. T."

"Not the TV series, the film. Liam Neeson and Bradley Cooper."

Grant picked up the Molotov cocktail and opened the door. The boiler room was pulsing with menace. The red light glared its warning.

"Well, don't forget. These fellas kill people for real. Bullets and knives don't leave flesh wounds. They rip you to pieces. Once you've done your bit, fall back to the rendezvous point."

Frevert proved again why he was so unsuitable for this. "The rendezvous point?"

Grant kept the impatience out of his voice. "The wheelie bins across the back."

Hope and Frevert gave the thumbs up. Grant nodded his approval and went out the door, along the passage towards the back stairs, then up the steps and out into the night.

03:55 HOURS

THE CAR PARK WAS three inches deep in snow. Grant stayed close to the building line as he eased his way around the compound, then passed the fire exit door. The security light picked out the falling snow like a swarm of white butterflies drifting from the night sky. In the outer reaches of the darkness they just became a shifting presence, something you sensed rather than saw, like the East Europeans up in the house. A danger to be addressed later.

Grant reached the corner and threw a quick glance along the side of the diner. The coast was clear. Whatever the gunmen were doing, they were doing it indoors. The van was still there with its doors open. The oil barrel jutted from the diner wall next to the drainpipe. There were questions that needed answering before he instigated the diversion. The answers were in a sack tied up in the barrel.

There were no windows between the corner and the drainpipe. Grant kept his back to the wall and edged towards the barrel. He wasn't sure how long it had been but he reckoned long enough for the midget to wake up. He fully expected to hear kicking and shouting from the sack, but there was no sound.

That was worrying. He didn't think he'd choked the little fella out so much that he'd gone to meet his maker. The other possibility was that he'd got out of the sack and gone to warn his mates. In that case, he'd be as dead as the rest of them and the gunmen would know there was a loose cannon on deck. Grant. That would change his plans. As of right now, the gunmen thought they were dealing with a bunch of local robbers and the catering staff. A chef and a waitress. If they'd got to the midget, then they'd know there was another. Like Luke Skywalker in *The Empire Strikes Back*. The dark side of the Force would be looking for Grant.

If they'd got to the midget.

Grant reached the barrel and looked inside. There was still no movement, but the sack hadn't gone. It wasn't empty either. He hesitated for a moment. He hoped he hadn't killed the midget. The sack was an inanimate object. Nothing moved except the snow that was building up on the top like icing on a cake. Then a sudden jerk of the canvas dislodged the snow and there was a sneeze from inside the sack.

Good. He was alive. Grant considered tipping him out of the barrel but then had a better idea. He wanted answers. He didn't want to be chasing the little fella around the car park to get them. Better to leave him in the barrel and apply the pressure from there. He put the petrol bomb down and leaned in to untie the sack. The wire was harsh and slippery with snow. He'd done such a good job of tying it up that untwisting the cable took a concerted effort. The man in the sack felt the activity and began to struggle. He shouted to be let out. Grant slammed his fist into the lump most likely to be the midget's head and told him to be quiet. He shut up and stopped struggling.

The top of the sack came open. A pale face with staring eyes peered out of the opening. Grant pulled the rag out of the bottle and held it over the barrel.

"Listen and be quiet."

"Go fuck yourself."

Grant should have known this fella wasn't going to be the kind of cute and cuddly dwarf they used in Santa's Grotto at Christmas. He was going to take a lot of persuading before he opened up. Grant didn't have time for persuading. A shortcut was needed. He emptied the bottle over the midget and pulled out the Zippo. The distinctive click of the lighter being opened focused the little fella's attention. Grant kept his voice low.

"I want answers, and I want them quick."

He jerked his head towards the diner.

"Your mates have been jumped by a bunch of East Europeans, and these boys came out with guns blazing. So don't give me any crap."

The man in the oil drum wiped petrol from his face. "Ukrainians."

"Drugs?"

The little man nodded. "Them, not us."

"So what's your game, then?"

"Tonight? Just to get the photos."

"How come they were in the diner safe?"

The little fella looked deflated. The gravity of his situation finally sunk in. His crew dead or captured. His only hope the big guy leaning over the oil drum. He let out a heavy sigh.

"They were copies. Ready for collection so the Ukrainians could keep the pressure on the councillor. We got a deal. Were told when the photos were being transferred from the big house to the diner."

Grant chose his next words carefully. Not a question, a statement.

"You bought the info."

The midget nodded. Grant continued.

"From the waitress."

Snow was settling on his shoulders. The bigger the flakes, the quieter the night became. The blizzard and the thick covering on the ground sucked all the sound out of the world. Grant waited for confirmation with a heavy heart. The response surprised him.

"Fuck no. The short-order cook."

Grant felt relief and disappointment. He'd misjudged Mickey Frevert.

"I thought he didn't know the combination."

"So what? He only had to tell us when the photos were in the safe."

"Your lads beat the shit out of him."

"I heard he tried to up the price. Anyway. It helps sell it to the girl. We didn't want anybody knowing who told us. We might use him again."

"Don't think that's gonna happen."

The weight of those words dampened the midget's spirits.

The weight of the revelation threw doubt into Grant's plan. If Frevert had been working for the robbers, would he still set the fuse of the pressure gauge? That was an important secondary diversion. Essential for them to get away once Grant had got Rivers out. He considered the possibilities and came down on the side of Frevert doing what he'd been told. His accomplices were dead. His best chance now was to throw in with Hope and Grant. The plan was still on.

Grant tipped the barrel over and the midget tumbled free. When he stood up, Grant realized he'd been doing the little fella a disservice. He wasn't that short after all. Only short compared to Grant.

"Things are gonna warm up around here. You'd better get your skates on."

"Skates?"

"Get the fuck out of here before I change my mind."

The little fella didn't need telling twice. Keeping out of sight from the diner windows, he ran across the car park and disappeared into the curtain of snow. Grant didn't wait to see him go. He went to the van and unscrewed the fuel cap. Using the petrol-soaked rag from the bottle, he shoved it down into the tank, then sparked the Zippo. The flame glowed orange in the cold blue light. The rag caught afire. Grant dashed round the back corner of the building and waited.

Two minutes later, the van exploded.

Grant opened the fire exit door and went inside.

04:05 HOURS

THE EXPLOSION BLASTED A ball of orange flame into the night and rattled the fittings of the corridor. All eyes in the diner would now be looking out of the front windows. Timing was everything. Grant sprinted down the corridor and stopped at the door to the food-preparation room.

The secret of positive action is to concentrate on your part and let the rest take care of itself. Mickey Frevert should be turning up the pressure on the boiler, then galloping across the snow to the wheelie bins. Jamie Hope should be making the emergency call from the rear office. Those were the other two parts of the plan. Grant couldn't worry about them. He had to focus on his part. The more dangerous part. Disabling two armed men and rescuing Wendy Rivers.

He wished the door had a porthole window like the one from the serving counter but had to console himself with knowing that nobody would be looking at the door from the corridor. He inched it open and saw two of the original robbers bound and gagged on the floor. There was no sign of Rivers. There was no sign of the gunmen either.

Keeping low, Grant entered the room and closed the door quietly. The two men on the floor were bruised and bleeding. Their hands were fastened behind their backs with heavy-duty cable ties not dissimilar to the ones police used at civil disturbances. One of them was the leader, his left eye swollen shut. The other Grant didn't recognize. Neither of them was the man with the limp and the car keys. Shame, but Grant reckoned he knew where the keys were.

First thing was to find Rivers.

Ignoring the men on the floor, he snuck a peek through the porthole window. The ball of flame had subsided to a shimmering blaze. It threw dancing shadows and an orange glow across the front windows. The tall, square-jawed Ukrainian stood at the front door, his head darting from side to side as he scanned the outside. The second Ukrainian held Wendy Rivers against the cash drawer of the open till. Both had a gun in one hand. Neither of them was holding it in the ready position. The threat was outside.

Grant checked the kitchen knives on the magnetic wall mount. The mount was empty. The Ukrainians had removed the temptation from the two detainees. Even though they were shackled by plastic bindings, there was no point giving them hope that they could cut their way free. Trouble was that also reduced Grant's choices. He didn't have time to start searching the drawers. The blazing distraction would only hold the Ukrainians' attention for so long.

He concentrated on the man holding Rivers against the till. He wasn't as tall as his colleague, but the muscles in his forearm bunched with effort as he held her tight. By contrast, his gun hand looked relaxed. Forefinger loose along the outside of the trigger guard. A confident stance that could instantly swing up for a snap shot or, if given more time, aim and shoot using his other hand for support.

Grant wasn't going to give him time.

A secondary explosion flared outside the windows. Cleaning fluids catching fire in the back of the van. The extra glare focused the two men's attention. Rivers slumped against the counter. Her captor stepped to one side to get a better view out the window.

The slight movement was all Grant needed. He opened the door and crossed the serving alley in two quick steps. Rivers saw him and couldn't keep it out of her eyes. The Ukrainian caught the flicker of recognition too late. Grant was right up behind him and clamping the gun hand in one fist before the man could react. Grant slipped his finger into the guard, twisted the arm backwards and up, and shot the man twice in the back.

"Down."

Grant's roar wasn't needed. Rivers dropped to the floor as soon as her arm was released. The Ukrainian by the front door spun round. His gun swung up in a short arc. His support hand slapped the butt as he took aim. Grant was already holding the dead man's gun and fired three times. The first was low. It caught the Ukrainian in the upper thigh. The second and third shots stitched a line across his chest, knocking him backwards through the window.

Grant was around the counter and running to the broken window before the man hit the snow in the car park. He went out the door and stood on the dying man's gun hand, clamping it to the ground. He didn't want the man throwing off a reflex shot or having a dead man's twitchy finger. Grant reached down and took the gun. He pressed the magazine release and dropped the magazine into his pocket. It was a match for the gun in his hand. He fired into the air to clear the chamber, then tossed the gun onto the roof.

Two down.

But he didn't know how many more were up at the house.

And he didn't know how long they'd stay up at the house after the explosion.

He glanced across the snowfield at the two parked cars. It was time to get the civilians to safety before waiting for the cavalry. Assuming Hope had got through on the phone. He trusted Jamie Hope. It was Mickey Frevert he was worried about. The pressure should be building in the boiler. No time to waste.

Rivers was cowering behind the counter when Grant came back inside. Her eyes betrayed fear and gratitude. Grant helped her up. She threw her arms around him, partly to stop from falling but mainly to feel the comfort of his presence. Grant patted her on the back and whispered in her ear.

"They thought you'd tipped off the robbers, didn't they?"

Rivers tensed in his arms. She leaned back to look into Grant's eyes as if gauging his reaction. She appeared to be reassured that he wasn't judging her but didn't answer. Grant answered for her.

"It was Mickey."

The flames were dying down outside. Grant had other things to worry about than hurting Rivers's feelings. The pressure should be building. When the boiler blew, it would take out half the diner and fire the floor safe like a mortar shell. Add to that the spilled petrol and the fuel store, and the explosion would make the van seem like small potatoes.

"I'll explain later. Let's get out of here."

He stepped back to see if Rivers could stand on her own. She wavered briefly but steadied herself. Grant pushed the food-preparation room door open and yanked the robbers to their feet. He didn't untie them. He didn't even want to take them with him but couldn't leave them to be blasted into heaven. What he did want was his car keys.

THE BLOOD SMEAR LEFT a trail along the corridor into the pantry. Grant sat the two survivors in the hallway and pointed the gun in their faces one at a time. He didn't need to speak. They got the message. He opened the pantry door and stood a sack of potatoes to hold it open. Keeping one eye on the two sitting on the floor he went into the pantry.

The two dead robbers were piled unceremoniously in the middle of the pantry. Grant didn't check for vital signs. They were as dead as anybody Grant had ever seen, and he'd seen plenty of dead people. He'd caused quite a few of those deaths but tried not to think about that. He found the man who'd taken the car keys and quickly searched him. Both sets of keys were in his coat pocket. Grant took them and stepped back into the corridor. He kicked the sack out of the way and let the pantry door close.

Wendy Rivers was still staring at the dead bodies even though the door had closed. Her eyes were wide and unmoving. She didn't blink. Grant laid a comforting hand across her shoulder and urged her towards the fire exit. The physical contact broke the spell, and she didn't need any further explanation. She led the way to the back door, Grant prodding the two robbers to their feet so they could follow.

A low rumbling began somewhere beneath their feet.

The distant humming built into a throbbing roar. Quiet at first but then growing louder. Frevert had done his bit. The boiler was overheating. Rivers reached the fire exit first. She burst through into the blizzard. Snow swirled into the corridor. In the short time it had taken for Grant to interrogate the midget, blow up the van, and neutralize the Ukrainians, the snow had gotten heavier. It would make using the cars more difficult. Snake Pass would be closed soon.

The rumbling became a physical presence.

It vibrated up through the floor.

Grant pushed the two robbers through the door and pointed to his right, beyond the fenced compound and into the gloom. The security light painted a semi-circle of dancing white demons but didn't reach more than twelve feet beyond the fire exit door. The wheelie bins were an invisible target, but at least Rivers knew where to find them.

Grant threw one last glance into the corridor as the pictures on the wall began to rattle and shake. One fell off its nail and smashed to the floor. The chain-hung fluorescent swayed, then one end came loose. It swung down and shattered against the wall. A window smashed.

He followed the others into the dark. The house was invisible up on the hill. Round the side of the diner, the van was almost burned out. Grant was halfway across the open ground when a deep thumping roar shook the ground. The boiler ripped apart and blasted shards of metal and plaster through the office floor. The concrete wasps' nest was fired into the sky. The petrol cans took the brunt of the blast, and then the fuel store exploded. The entire back end of Woodlands Truck Stop and Diner disappeared in a gigantic ball of flame and splintered wood.

04:15 HOURS

Hope and Frevert were waiting for them behind the wheelie bins. The chef threw a nervous glance at the two robbers, then pretended he didn't know them. Grant thought it was best to get this out in the open.

"Master chef. Look at me."

His tone was harsh to get Frevert's attention, but he changed it to borderline friendly once their eyes locked.

"I'm gonna cut you some slack. I don't care that you sold 'em the info about the photos. And I don't blame you for the slack-jawed, nasty bastards they turned out to be. But four men are dead, and if you don't do what I tell you, I'm gonna punch your nose through the back of your head. Understand?"

Frevert nodded. Rivers looked sheepish. Hope didn't waste time asking what that was all about. He held one hand up to the side of his face in the shape of a telephone.

"I got through to Sergeant Ballhaus. He's going to mobilize the local division and the armed response vehicle—their whole team."

"Good work."

Grant stuck the gun down the back of his belt and rested a hand on Frevert's shoulder.

"You too. Well done."

He looked over the top of the wheelie bins at the inferno that had once been the boiler room and management office. The main corridor and fire exit had gone. The flat roof across the rear section of the truck stop had been splintered upwards around the gaping hole. Flames licked at the wood. The cellar and fuel store was a blazing crater at the heart of the volcano. Grant barely gave it a second glance. He was looking beyond the diner to the front car park. He took the two bunches of car keys out of his pocket and locked eyes with Hope.

"Time to get this lot out of here."

He handed Hope one set of keys.

"What's yours like in the snow?"

"Front-wheel drive. Handles pretty good."

"We'll use your car, then. Mine's for shit in this stuff."

Grant pointed at Hope, then jerked a thumb towards the diner. "You take the lead. Stay left, away from the light. I'll bring up the rear."

There was no further discussion. Hope walked out from behind the wheelie bins and took a diagonal course away from the flames, skirting the end of the diner that was still intact. Rivers and Frevert followed. Grant nudged the two robbers to join the line and kept close behind them. He doubted they'd try and make a run for it in this snow but wasn't going to take the chance.

Darkness and the blizzard swallowed them up. Grant was hopeful this would be over soon. It wasn't until they reached the cars that he realized it wasn't going to be as easy as that.

THE FLOOR SAFE AND its cement cocoon had fired through the ceiling like a mortar, and just like a mortar it had followed a similar trajectory. Up high at first, then arcing forward until gravity brought it back to earth. Right onto the bonnet of Jamie Hope's car. The engine steamed as the improvised mortar shell cooled. The radiator hissed water vapor into the night. A pool of oil darkened the ground.

Hope stared at his wrecked car in disbelief.

"I guess we'll use yours, then."

Grant was way ahead of him. He stepped round the back of the Mondeo and opened the boot. He took the toolbox out and put it on the back seat, then dragged the first robber by the arm.

"In."

The robber who had once been the leader hesitated. Grant nudged him against the bumper until he overbalanced and toppled into the boot. The second robber got the message. He climbed in under his own power. Grant slammed the lid down, then told Rivers and Frevert to get in. They climbed in the back seat, either side of the toolbox. Grant handed Hope the keys.

"Handles like a slippery fuck in the snow. Take it easy. Turn right onto the main road. That's where they'll be coming from."

"The ARVs?"

"Everybody. Local station is over that way."

Hope looked at the keys in his hand, then back at Grant.

"Aren't you coming?"

Grant shook his head. "Somebody's got to guide them in when they arrive."

"I'll stay with you."

"No, you won't. I need you to take care of them."

Hope looked crestfallen. His shoulders sagged.

"I want to go charging in with my warrant card."

"And getting them to cease and desist. I know. But what did I tell you? No radios and no backup. Well, backup's on the way. They'll reach you first. Give 'em the heads up before they get to me."

Hope seemed to take heart from that.

Grant patted him on the back. "Consider this your first patrol out of company. Single crewed."

Their eyes locked, and Grant could see the pride welling up inside his young probationer. Jamie Hope was going to make one helluva fine police officer. Grant slapped the roof of the car.

"Now let's get this show on the road."

They didn't shake hands. They didn't give each other a manly hug. They simply nodded at each other, then got on with the job. Hope slid into the driver's seat and turned the ignition. The engine coughed but wouldn't start. He turned the key again. Same result. He stared through the windscreen at Grant and held his hands up in mock surrender.

Grant mimicked turning the key again. "Doesn't like the cold."

He kicked the front wing.

Hope turned the ignition again and this time the engine roared into life. He gently engaged reverse to ease the Mondeo out of the snowy ruts it had settled into. The car moved backwards. The wheels crawled slowly. Then they spun out of control in the deep snow.

The Mondeo was front-wheel drive too but had never been good in the snow. The drive wheels skidded sideways and buried themselves deeper in the drift that had built up along one side of the car. Grant leaned on the bonnet and tried to push, but his feet couldn't get purchase in the snow. He glanced at his shoes. He'd got so used the snowfall that he hadn't paid attention to how heavy the blizzard had become. His feet disappeared six inches into the fluffy white covering. That meant it was maybe seven or eight inches deep, allowing for the compacted snow beneath his hi-tech Magnums.

Hope tried forward drive. The wheels spun again, burying the tires deeper into the snow. He tried reverse, then forward, then reverse again, attempting to rock the car loose from the icy grip. All that did was skid the car to one side, then the other. Steam rose from the burning rubber. The compacted snow melted, then turned to ice. After a few minutes, Grant slapped the roof. Hope turned the engine off. This car wasn't going anywhere.

Grant kicked the wheel.

"Shit."

He glanced back at the diner and froze.

"Double shit."

Beyond the diner, up the hill in the distance, half a dozen lights flickered across the snow. Torches. Coming this way. More Ukrainians. More guns. Grant slapped the roof again and glared at Hope.

"Out of the car. Now."

04:25 HOURS

GRANT LEFT THE TWO robbers locked in the boot. There was no point dragging extra baggage through the snow. The pinpoints of torchlight had skirted the tree line on the hill and were coming down the road from the house. Not a very good pattern for a search party but well grouped for reinforcements. They were heading straight for the diner. Coming at it from the access road meant they were on the same side as the burnt-out van. Grant led his group around the opposite side in a wide loop, keeping their trail of footprints as far away from the building as possible. He doubted the Ukrainians would make a wide sweep. Not once they found Bohdan and Marko in the restaurant.

Grant had never served in the Ukraine but had seen action in various parts of Eastern Europe. His experience was that they weren't as excitable as the natives of the desert countries but they could still be volatile under the right circumstances. Finding two of their friends shot to death in the diner could provoke volatile. Their reaction would be one of two things. They'd either go off in a rage and shoot anything that moved or they'd make a systematic search of the building.

Either way, Grant didn't want to be anywhere near the diner when the bodies were found. If he'd thought about it earlier, he could have arranged the corpses to look like they'd shot it out with the two dead robbers, but Grant had left their bodies in the pantry. No way even a hotheaded Ukrainian was going to believe there'd been a shootout like that.

Good thing was the Ukrainians didn't know how many robbers there'd been, so they wouldn't be looking for the other two. Bad thing was they had been told to finish the chef and the waitress. The chef and the waitress weren't among the dead. So they'd definitely search the diner and check for footprints leading away. The heavy snow would help Grant there. It had been a long time since they'd dashed from the fire exit to the wheelie bins. Since then, they'd avoided the buildings en route to the cars and the same coming back. The wheelie bins didn't feel safe anymore, though.

Keeping to the southern edge of the car park, Grant found an outcrop of rocks with pine trees across the top. It was the best shelter he could find. There were no other outbuildings, and even if there were they would be the first place the gunmen would search. Grant guided Rivers and Frevert into the shelter and immediately felt relief from the blizzard. Hope followed them in, and they all crouched in a huddle against the rock. The canopy of trees overhead kept the snow at bay. It even felt warmer out of the blizzard, comparatively speaking.

Frevert's teeth were chattering.

Rivers hugged herself but couldn't stop the shivering.

They might be protected from the elements, but this wasn't going to warm them up. Grant slipped his leather coat off and draped it around Rivers' shoulders. He signaled for Frevert to join her under the cover.

"No time for being shy. Keep each other warm."

He turned to Hope and jerked his chin towards the diner. The orange glow of the flames had died down in the crater. Falling snow was turning to rain above the heat from the fire. Not heavy enough to put it out but sufficient to dampen the roof and walls.

"The fire's not going to spread. Those fellas are gonna be pissed off when they find their mates. They're gonna tear the place apart looking for who did it. But once they come up empty handed, they'll head back up to the house. They've got a delivery to unload."

He rested an arm across Hope's shoulders. "Once they've gone, you can get back in the warmth."

Hope looked at his tutor.

"You might as well get warm too. We can guide backup in together."

Grant shook his head.

"I want the civilians out of here. This place is gonna go weapons hot as soon as the ARVs arrive. I don't want innocent bystanders getting caught in the crossfire."

He looked out from the shelter. The diner was barely visible through the curtain of snowflakes dancing across the night. The two cars had completely disappeared. The Transit van was a smouldering wreck. The lack of wind meant the snow was floating straight down so there was no drifting up the side of the diner. That would be the same coming down the access road from the house. The reinforcements would encounter little resistance in their march towards the diner.

Even as Grant considered that, he saw flickering torchlight clear the bottom of the road. He counted six men. They began to spread out once they were clear of the restrictions of the road. Three moved along the back of the diner. The other three disappeared around the far side.

Grant turned to Hope. "Stay put until they've all gone."

"What about you?"

Grant nodded towards the invisible cars. "Mondeo might be shit in the snow." Then he jerked his head up towards the house. "But the trucks that went up the hill sounded big and ugly. Means they're gonna have big, ugly tires. Better traction even in deep snow."

Hope smiled his understanding.

Grant continued.

"And if I get one before they unload it, we're gonna need more evidence bags than back at Edgebank Close."

"Then can we get them to cease and desist?"

"As soon as backup arrives. Yes."

He looked at the shivering bundle under his leather coat. Encouraging words were pointless but he gave them anyway.

"We'll get you out of here soon. PC Hope'll look after you till then."

Grant threw one last glance towards the diner, then left the shelter and turned right. He followed the edge of the car park until he found the gentle slope he'd gone up almost two hours ago, then began to climb.

04:35 HOURS

THE HOUSE WASN'T IN darkness anymore. It was lit up like a Christmas tree. Any pretence at being uninhabited had been discarded when the Ford Transit had blown up and the rear of the diner had been destroyed. After that, pretending the house was empty seemed a little pointless.

Grant kept to the tree line as he skirted the house. The ground floor windows were all lit. Lights were on in the front bedroom over the porch roof and two of the windows around the side. None of that posed a problem. It meant that whoever was inside the house wouldn't be able to see shit-all in the darkness outside the windows. What did pose a problem was the security lights on the exterior walls he'd missed before. A brilliant white ring of light surrounded the house. It highlighted the dancing flakes like white particles in a freshly shaken snow globe.

Even under the trees the snow was ankle deep. That combined with the low branches and the ongoing blizzard sucked all the sound out of the night. There might well be movement inside the house, but there was no sound at all outside. The silence made Grant's breath sound loud in his ears.

He watched and listened from under the trees. He'd missed the security lights because they were under the eaves, high on each corner. The first thing that suggested was CCTV cameras. Grant scoured the walls from the ground up to the eaves. No cameras. Good. Since this was a drug distribution center, he doubted the dealers would want recordings of their illegal activity. The lights were a defense mechanism, not a crime prevention device. They weren't worried about being burgled because the house was never empty and the occupants were armed to the teeth.

The lights did mean that Grant had to make a wider arc as he circled the house towards the underground garage entrance. Keeping to the trees all the way round, he kept his eyes peeled for movement in the snow. He wasn't foolish enough to believe they'd sent their entire force down to the diner. They weren't going to leave three truckloads of smuggled drugs unguarded.

The thing was to find the trucks.

Another thing was trucks don't fit into an underground domestic garage.

That should make finding them easy.

Grant was around the side of the house now. He could see in through the kitchen windows. Two men were drinking from steaming mugs. Somebody else was moving in the hallway near the cellar door. There was no sound of engines running. There was no sound of doors slamming. All the movement was inside the house.

Snow crunched beneath Grant's boots as he moved farther to his right. The trees stopped short of an expanse of virgin snow. Maybe a garden or play area. The garden ended at the edge of a ridge that overlooked darkness beyond the security lights' reach. Darkness always intrigued Grant. You couldn't hide three heavy-duty trucks in the light, but shadows could hide anything.

He moved towards the ridge. There was no cover anymore, just the dark at the edge of the light. Grant kept low and moved slow, not wanting to stand out. He eased towards the overlook and knelt in the snow. His breath plumed around his head. His heart thumped in his chest. It pulsed in his ears.

The trucks were parked in a wide turnaround, line abreast, facing the house. They were large ex-army wagons with green canvas covers and drop-down tailgates. Grant had been right. They were big and ugly. And they had big and ugly tires. He wondered if they'd left the keys in the ignition. There was only one way to find out. He sidled over the edge and made his way into the shadows.

THE FIRST TRUCK WAS unlocked, but he didn't open the door. He was conscious that the trucks were facing the house and that opening the door would trigger the interior light. The shadows might well keep the trucks hidden, but the light would stand out like a beacon in the night. He didn't want to do that until he was certain the keys had been left in.

He went to the driver's window and closed his eyes, counted to five, then opened them again. After the total blackout, the dark interior of the cab was almost like daylight. The interior was clean and tidy. There was no rubbish or papers or cigarette butts littering the dashboard. There was nothing that might leave a clue as to who the driver was. Nothing that could provide DNA evidence. Nothing with a name or an address or a point of origin. These fellas were playing it very safe.

The ignition chamber glinted silver in the gloom. Grant focused on that. The keys hadn't been left in. There was no key fob dangling from the ignition. He scanned the flat indentations on the dashboard, the traditional storage place for anything left in the cab. Nothing. The other possibility was the sun visor above the driver's side of the windscreen. It was folded up against the roof. Grant remembered Arnold Schwarzenegger finding the spare keys there in *Terminator 2* but doubted that Ukrainian drug smugglers would be so foolish.

He quickly checked the other trucks. They were the same. Unlocked. No keys. No evidence. Sun visors folded shut against the cab roofs. He concentrated on the visors to see if they were fully closed. If somebody hid the keys behind the visors, there would be a bulge preventing them from lying flat against the ceiling. There were no bulges. He didn't want to risk the interior light just yet but he wanted to be certain. At least in one of the trucks. He chose the one farthest from the house. The truck was angled slightly, giving the driver's door some protection from prying eyes. Using the point of his elbow, he smashed the glass. It disintegrated into a thousand diamond-hard cubes. Spots of blood beaded on his shirtsleeve around the elbow, but he ignored them. The pain was minimal.

Climbing on the stepping plate and the mudguard, he reached up and flicked the sun visor down. There was nothing hidden behind it. Point proved. They'd taken the keys in with them. Something else troubled him, though. He knew the trucks were parked behind the Ukrainians' house in the middle of nowhere, but leaving them unlocked and unattended with millions of pounds' worth of drugs seemed risky for a gang who were eliminating their risks.

He went round the back of the farthest truck. It reminded him of his army days. Traveling in the back of a military transport with the heavy equipment and the canvas flapping in the wind. The drop-down tailgate was latched at either end, with a sturdy three-rung ladder welded to the chassis. The green canvas was laced along both sides and across the bottom with thick cord.

They hadn't unloaded yet.

Grant hauled himself up on the bottom rung of the ladder.

The cord was pulled tight and securely knotted. He tried to gauge how long it had been since the trucks arrived. Maybe an hour. A bit less. Not long enough to unload three large trucks and transfer the goods into the house. Even if they had removed the delivery, they wouldn't have retied the canvas so tight. He checked the ground at the back of the truck. The only footprints were his. He dropped from the ladder and checked the other trucks. Same thing. No disturbance of the snow. Even allowing for some filling by the fresh snow, there would be some signs of activity. From all three trucks, the only indentations led from the cab towards the house.

This could be a bonus. If Grant could start one of the trucks, he'd have all the evidence he'd need for the biggest drug bust in history. Forget Lee Adkins's bath panel hideaway. This would trump the Edgebank Close seizure that Adkins was going to walk free of. With ARVs on the way, the Ukrainians weren't going to be walking anywhere.

Grant hopped up onto the ladder again and began to untie the rope. He slackened the cord and peeled open a corner of the canvas. It was dark inside. The cavernous interior was just a huge square block of darkness. He unfastened another two feet of canvas and pulled it back. He closed his eyes again, counted to five, then viewed the interior with his night vision.

The cargo bay was empty. Not only empty but as clean and tidy as the cab up front. There were no boxes of drugs. There were no sacks of ingredients. There was none of the dust or crap or debris associated with a recently unloaded truck.

Grant shut the flap and dropped to the ground. He checked the other trucks. He didn't need to open the canvas as far as the first one. They were both empty. They were both clean. The snow was beginning to fill his footprints, but no amount of snow was going to disguise the fact that he'd been there. It couldn't hide the men who should have unloaded the trucks either. It hadn't disguised the drivers' trails from the cabs to the house. A triple thread that became a single trail as they approached the house. Nobody had come out to greet them. Nobody had helped unload the trucks. Because the trucks hadn't brought anything to the house. Whatever they had delivered, they'd dropped it somewhere else and cleaned up the evidence.

The question was, where?

Grant put the disappointment behind him. No point worrying about what you can't control. Instead he focused on what he could control: finding the keys and getting the civilians to safety. The keys were in the house. It was time to find the driver and borrow his truck.

04:45 HOURS

GRANT TRUDGED THROUGH THE snow towards the house. He approached along the bottom of the ridge that protected him from the security light until he was almost at the sloping drive into the underground garage. He paused at the edge of the shadows. There were no fresh tire tracks into or out of the garage. Nothing that hadn't been there when he'd climbed in through the toilet window. The faint tracks he'd seen then were completely filled in now.

There was something he hadn't noticed the first time, though. Along one side of the ramp, three air vents stuck out of the snow like metal funnels with conical lids the shape of a Chinaman's hat. They reminded Grant of one of his favorite films, *The Dirty Dozen*. The air vents along the side of the chateau. Lee Marvin and the others had forced them open to drop grenades and petrol down. In the film, the vents led to an underground bunker where the German generals were hiding. He wondered what the Ukrainians were hiding two floors underground. One floor below the basement and internal garage.

He noticed something else as well.

On either side of the doublewide garage door.

The ramp narrowed as it reached the door, and there was a drop-off on each side, three feet wide and about twelve inches lower than the drive. At the base of the wall in the left-hand drop-off, almost completely blocked by drifting snow, were two narrow slit windows. The glass had been covered from the inside, but the edge of one cover had peeled away. Bright yellow light spilled across the snow.

Grant waited in the shadows as he inspected the valley formed by the bottom of the ramp. It was a dead end with no other way out. Going down there to check the windows would leave him exposed if somebody came round behind him. He glanced up at the house. There was no movement that he could see. There was no sound of doors opening or approaching footsteps in the snow. He decided to risk it.

After one last look around him, he slid down the embankment to the bottom of the ramp. Snow crunched underfoot. It sounded loud in the fluffy silence of the night. His breath formed a cloud around his head. He dropped to his knees and cut a wedge of snow out of the drift, exposing the rest of the narrow window. The internal covering looked like black paper pasted to the glass. The triangle that had peeled off the corner was only a couple of inches wide. He leaned forward and peered through the gap.

The window was high up in the subbasement, probably running along the top of the wall at ceiling level. It didn't provide a good angle for looking down into the room. Something large and square stood just below the window and blocked his view. All that he could see was a sliver of floor space and some kind of industrial machinery. Shadows moved around the edges of his vision. There was a lot of activity down there, but he couldn't tell what it was.

He leaned back to see if there was any light from the other window. There wasn't.

The nearest vent was just behind him. He shuffled up to it and listened. There was clanking and scuffling and muffled voices in a foreign language. Grant didn't speak Ukrainian, but the tone was affable, with the occasional laugh. Men at work. But doing what?

He looked at the windows to the subbasement, then glanced at the air vents. It sounded like most of the activity was down there and not in the garage. He went over and put an ear to the double-wide door just in case. Silence apart from echoes from down below. He ticked off the layout and movement in his mind.

First floor. Couple of lights on in the bedrooms but no movement.

Ground floor. Men in the kitchen and hallway.

Basement garage. No sound of movement.

Subbasement. Lots of activity.

He scrambled back up the banking from the ramp and melted into the shadows. The ridge protected him from the light again. Somewhere behind him the trucks waited in the dark. Somewhere in the house the drivers had the keys. Grant had seen at least two men drinking hot drinks in the kitchen and a third wandering around in the hallway. The sort of thing lorry drivers did while waiting for instructions. They didn't seem to be hanging together. Grant hoped he'd be able to catch one of them on his own.

One final check of the perimeter, then he moved towards the back door.

THE KITCHEN LIGHTS HELPED in two ways. They lit the inside of the house so Grant could see every corner of the kitchen and they blasted the reflection of that interior back at anyone trying to look out the windows. The security lights around the house negated some of that but not enough that the men drinking coffee or whatever it was could get a good look outside. Grant was counting on that but erred towards caution anyway.

He kept below the window level and hugged the building line as he crept past the kitchen. He'd glanced in through the window near the back door and seen that the hallway was clear. Once he reached the far side of the kitchen, he risked a glance in the end window and saw three empty mugs steaming on the drainer beside the kitchen sink. The drivers had finished warming themselves and gone down to the basement. That was good and bad. Good because it meant Grant could sneak in the back door. Bad because he'd have to go downstairs to get a set of keys.

Then he caught movement out of the corner of his eye. An orange jacket through the adjoining door to the living room. Next to the drop-leaf table at the front window. The ashtray. The man was having a smoke at the house's equivalent of the unofficial smoking area.

Grant didn't wait. He went straight to the back door. The footprints leading up from the parked trucks stopped here and had already begun to fill in. The door wasn't locked. He closed it quietly behind him and turned left into the kitchen. Kept close to the wall as he sidled to the living room door. Ducked his head round the open door to get his bearings. The man had his back to the kitchen. He was looking out of the front window and tapping ash into the ashtray. Grant could see the silhouette of the kitchen door reflected in the glass.

Not good.

But the man seemed to be enjoying his cigarette. He turned his head to one side, closed his eyes, and blew smoke at the ceiling.

Good.

Grant slipped into the lounge, keeping the man's back to him. The house was a solid detached property with sturdy floorboards. Reinforced because of the two levels beneath it. The living room carpet helped. There was no sound as Grant quickly crossed the room and locked one arm around the smoker's neck and one hand over his mouth, mashing the cigarette into his teeth. There was a brief muffled exclamation before Grant yanked the head sharply to the left. The crack of breaking bones was sharp and vicious.

The man dropped like a rag doll. Grant lowered him to the ground and quickly checked behind him. Nobody else had come in. He suddenly realized how cold he'd become. He checked the dead man's pockets and found a big solid key on a worn leather fob. The driver wasn't armed. Grant unzipped the orange windcheater and pulled it off the man's shoulders. It was a perfect fit. The lining was still warm. He zipped it closed and put the key in his pocket.

The body lay on the floor in front of the table. Grant glanced around the room for a hiding place but there wasn't one. He checked the drop-leaf table. The table flap was almost the height of the table. It reached a few inches from the floor. That would do. He raised the flap, rolled the body under the table, then dropped the flap again. For added disguise he pulled one of the dining chairs round the front and angled it next to the ashtray. He felt a twinge of guilt and sadness at having killed the driver but quickly rationalized it. The Ukrainians had ordered Wendy's death. This guy was guilty by association. It wasn't like tying up a midget in a barrel.

Time to get the hell out of there. He'd achieved his objective and got a key to the truck. All he needed to do now was start it up and charge down the access road to pick up the three waiting for him in the makeshift shelter. And be quick about it before the Ukrainians heard the engine and came out to investigate. The trucks were big and heavy but weren't built for speed. There might be more gunmen in the subbasement. All they'd need to do was come out of the garage ramp and cut him off as he drove past. Bang, bang, you're dead.

That was one problem. The other was that Grant really wanted to see what they were doing in the subbasement before he left. A diversion would help alleviate both problems. Get the Ukrainians charging upstairs while Grant dashed out of the garage ramp after a quick recce downstairs.

He looked through the kitchen door at the electric cooker. The best plans are the simplest. He was already unloading the spare clip into his hands as he walked through the door. He turned one of the cooker rings on full, dropped the bullets into the frying pan, and stood it on the ring.

04:50 HOURS

THERE IS NO EXACT science for how long it takes a bullet to heat up and explode. Grant had seen bullets dropped in a campfire take fifteen minutes before going ballistic. Then again, he'd also seen a single bullet dropped onto the hot desert floor go off almost immediately. Bullets are designed to fit snugly in the chamber and only ignite at the thump of the firing pin. Used that way, they nearly always went off when you wanted them to.

Bullets in a frying pan, Grant had never tried before.

He reckoned he'd have between now and sometime later. Not an exact science.

He didn't wait to find out. The only thing he knew was he wanted to be down the first flight of stairs before the alarm sounded and bullets began ricocheting round the kitchen. He was at the wood-panelled door before the smell of hot metal drifted into the hallway.

He listened at the door. Remembered how noisy the footsteps coming up from the garage had sounded before. There were no footsteps now. He opened the door and had a quick look down the stairway. Nobody there. He snaked his hand around the butt of the gun, then took it away again. He hated guns. Hadn't liked them even when he was in the army. That's why he told everyone he'd been a typist—to deflect any questions about his military service. He didn't like them, but there comes a time when you've got to put your feelings aside and do the right thing. The right thing now was to be armed and dangerous before walking down those stairs.

He drew the gun and checked there was a round in the chamber.

Stepped through the door and stood at the top of the stairs.

From the hallway the door looked like a storage cupboard. From the top step it didn't look much bigger. There was just enough headroom for him to stand upright, but the sloping roof followed the stairs all the way down, and if he ducked his head forward he'd be scraping his forehead for twenty feet. To go down standing he had to lean back slightly and that meant he was off-balance. Short of going down on his backside, there was no alternative. He was down four of the steps before he felt comfortable. By the time he reached the bottom, he could have balanced on a washing line. Grant was a very quick learner.

The door at the bottom was full size and open. Keeping his gun hand loose, he risked a look round the corner. The garage was marginally wider than the up-and-over door. Big enough for a two-car family, with plenty of room to spare. The only car in there now was a mud-splattered Mercedes with dents and scrapes down one side. It was parked facing in. The metallic grey car stood in a puddle of water but was mainly dry. Any snow it had brought in had melted a long time ago. Grant laid one hand on the bonnet. The engine was cold.

The keys were in the ignition.

The tires were heavy-duty snow Pirellis.

Good to know. Maybe he wouldn't need the truck after all. He opened the door and took the keys. Closed it with a barely audible click. There was a lot of clutter in the basement. Things hanging from the walls. Storage cupboards. A workbench with tools scattered on top. A dumbwaiter hatch on the back wall. Two large fuel oil drums for the generator that pulsed in the corner. The truck stop and the house were a long way off the national grid. Independent power was essential. The overhead fluorescent was bright and harsh. The yellow light from the subbasement was a touch warmer. Grant could see it spilling up from the stairwell in the far corner.

The garage floor was poured concrete to accommodate the weight of two cars. That meant that the subbasement was over to one side and stretched outwards under the air vents beside the ramp. Not a massive room, judging by the vents. Grant walked across to the concrete steps but kept his distance. Noted the stack of cardboard boxes at the top of the stairs. He used the hosepipe on the wall and the battered metal cupboard for cover and peered over the edge of the stairwell.

The door at the bottom was open. The activity down there was louder despite the noise from the generator. The contents of the boxes became clear. Grant watched as faceless men packed plastic bags of white powder into identical boxes in the utility room. Not the dealer bags he'd found under Lee Adkins's bathtub, but the larger bags that Adkins had filled them from. Like five-pound bags of sugar, only you wouldn't want this in your tea. Adkins had three of them under the bath. The subbasement looked like it could supply a thousand Lee Adkinses.

Grant leaned against the wall and let out a sigh.

The generator rumbled on.

The voices continued their banter downstairs.

Grant felt the truck key in his pocket. The empty truck that was part of a three-vehicle convoy. Not to deliver smuggled drugs to the house behind Woodlands Truck Stop and Diner but to distribute them from the integral garage beneath it. They weren't smuggling drugs into the country. They were manufacturing them here and exporting them around the world. No wonder a local councillor in your pocket was a good thing to have. A local councillor with responsibility for import and export controls in the north of England. And a local councillor caught on camera having his cock sucked in a back-street hotel.

Grant was considering that when an electric motor began to whine in the distance. There was a sudden chill and a flurry of snow as the up-and-over garage door slowly crawled open.

THE BATTERED METAL CUPBOARD felt cold and insubstantial. The workbench was more solid but not as tall. It was just behind Grant in the corner near the generator. There was enough of a gap between the two for him to crouch down and hide. He backed against the wall and ducked his head behind a gnarled metal vice and a G-clamp. He reached across the workbench for a large tin of Swarfega and positioned it in front of his face, then settled to wait the newcomers out.

The door crawled open at a snail's pace.

Six inches from the ground.

Twelve inches.

Snow drifted three feet across the floor and swirled in tiny eddies.

Eighteen inches.

Two feet.

Three pairs of snow-covered boots came into view. The hit team returning from the diner. Grant hoped they'd go straight down into the subbasement to make their report. Either that or straight up to the kitchen for a hot drink. He consulted the timer in his head. Five minutes since he'd come down here. The frying pan would be heating up pretty good. If they went upstairs, they'd be facing hot lead by the time they put the kettle on. Worst-case scenario, they'd discover the bullets and turn off the cooker. No matter. By then Grant would be out of the garage door and halfway to the trucks with their big ugly tires.

The door continued along the ceiling track as it was drawn up and over by the electric motor. Another two pairs of boots came into view. That made five out of six. A door slammed upstairs—a long way upstairs. One of the bedrooms. Somebody keeping watch from the highest point? If that was the case, it would have been from one of the unlit windows. A decent view across the hillside to the flames at the diner. The neon sign had gone out when the boiler exploded. It would be the fire that guided the ARVs like a beacon in the night. That and Jamie Hope waving them in when they arrived.

The door was halfway open. The five pairs of boots became five pairs of legs, crawling up to five waistbands. Falling snow danced in the overhead fluorescent and settled on the garage floor. The light spilled out across the ramp. Three more pairs of legs came into view behind the first five. That didn't add up. They were different to the other legs. Not heavily padded dark trousers and boots.

The whine of the engine grew louder in Grant's ears.

His heartbeat thumped like somebody hitting him in the chest.

He held his breath.

The wood-panelled door in the ground floor hallway opened and footsteps sounded on the stairs, coming fast.

The garage door stopped at the end of the ceiling track. The snow outside was coming down heavier, obscuring the five gunmen and their three captives until they stepped into the garage. The sixth gunman brought up the rear and pressed the wall button to close the door. The engine kicked into reverse.

Frevert and Rivers were shivering. They stamped their feet and rubbed their arms to get warm. Jamie Hope held his handkerchief against a cut down one side of his face. He looked embarrassed and defeated, as if he'd let everyone down. Grant wanted to reassure him but kept his position beside the workbench. Until the voice called over from the bottom of the stairs.

"Come out with your hands in the air."

Six guns swung towards Grant from the garage entrance and a seventh from the other side of the workbench. Grant recognized the voice. It was the man who'd sent Bohdan and Marko to finish the chef and the waitress. His gun was pointing at the tin of Swarfega in front of Grant's face.

Grant stood up and put his gun on the workbench. "They only say that in the movies."

The lead Ukrainian didn't smile. He squeezed the trigger and fired.

04:55 HOURS

THE TIN OF SWARFEGA exploded in a shower of green gel. The bullet split the tin, scored a groove in the heavy wood of the workbench, and buried itself in the wall behind Grant. The Ukrainian still didn't smile.

"They do that in the movies too?"

Grant couldn't remember seeing anyone shoot a tin of Swarfega at the pictures, but this wasn't the time to mention it. These men were all business. They were armed and dangerous and not to be messed with. Grant slowly raised his hands in the air.

The Ukrainian nodded. "That's better."

He glanced at the bedraggled captives from the diner, then back at Grant.

"You and your friends have been busy. I do not approve of your activities."

Grant kept his tone calm and level. "Those fellas with the bats were robbing the place."

Calm seemed to be the Ukrainian's default setting. "Yes, they were, weren't they? Let's talk about that, shall we?"

He moved away from the workbench and stood in the middle of the garage. The grey Mercedes took up half the floor space. The huddle of captives surrounded by Ukrainian gunmen stood in front of the up-and-over door. Grant stood beside the tall metal storage cupboard, two paces out of his hiding place. He appeared calm and relaxed on the outside, but inside he was angry and pissed off. His mind raced as he tried to calculate time and distance—the distance to snatch his gun from the workbench and the time it would take to shoot the Ukrainian mouthpiece.

The other thing running through his mind was heat and conductivity. How much heat would be conducted through the shell casings before the bullets started exploding? He'd been down here ten minutes. Shouldn't be long now.

None of that showed on Grant's face.

The lead Ukrainian stepped in front of the captives. He held a hand up to one of the gunmen, who took a large creased envelope out of his coat. He didn't open it or hand it over. Everyone knew what was inside.

"They chose tonight of all nights to rob a back-road diner in the middle of nowhere. The only night that these photographs were in the floor safe. That is quite a coincidence, wouldn't you agree?"

Grant didn't answer.

Frevert's teeth continued to chatter with the cold.

Hope and Rivers stood in silence.

The Ukrainian continued. "And they took this envelope out of a locked safe without having to break it open—as if they knew the combination. Another coincidence, perhaps?"

Rivers shuddered, her eyes widening at the implication.

Grant felt his blood begin to boil. He kept his face impassive.

"There was no choice. We had to open it for them."

Cold grey eyes stared at Grant. "There is always a choice." His hand tightened around the pistol grip. "Some choose to mind their own business."

His finger slipped into the trigger guard. "And some choose to sell information that was not theirs to sell."

He slowly raised the gun. "Inviting low-life scum and robbers into the diner to take what does not belong to them."

Rivers tensed. Grant relaxed. He took half a step towards the workbench. He thought he could smell hot metal drifting down from the kitchen. Time and distance. It would be tight. He flexed his shoulders. Relaxed his knees. Prepared to move fast. Before he even managed to move, he knew he would be too late.

Wendy Rivers stared across the room at him.

The Ukrainian snapped the gun into firing position.

The gunshots sounded loud in the enclosed space.

Mickey Frevert was shot three times in the chest.

GRANT ALMOST DIVED FOR his gun on the workbench, but six Ukrainian gunmen had other ideas. Their gun arms zeroed him like spokes to the center of a wheel. He had no chance of reaching the gun before dropping like Frevert. He didn't need to try. Rivers was out of immediate danger.

The burning metal smell grew stronger.

The lead Ukrainian turned towards Grant. "That leaves us with one waitress and two off-duty policemen."

Grant weighed his options. They were extremely limited. Stay put and die or go for the gun and die. He needed to delay those outcomes to allow time for option number three. Best delaying tactic he'd ever known was to use the coppers' most potent weapon: stay calm and talk. The Ukrainian didn't seem averse to talking.

"Now what do you suggest we do about that?"

Grant took his cue. "You can let us go, and I'll put in a good word for you at court."

"A good word about what?"

Grant kept his arms loose. "About the distribution of enough drugs to supply a small country and the cold-blooded murder of an innocent bystander."

The Ukrainian lowered the gun and waved it around to emphasise his point. "You saw that, huh? And the latest shipment?"

Grant nodded.

"I'll count to ten and give you a head start."

The Ukrainian swept his gun hand to include Hope, Rivers, and Grant.

"So that would make you witnesses to my crimes. Might be better if I disposed of you instead. What do you say?"

Grant looked at Wendy Rivers. Her eyes were wide with fear. He moved on to Jamie Hope and focused on the probationer for a few seconds. Hope glanced behind him at the wall button, then back to Grant, proving once again that he was a prospect for the future. Grant needed to insure he had a future. He turned his attention back to the Ukrainians' leader.

"I'd say that killing a couple of armed robbers and their snitch was a whole lot different to shooting two off-duty police officers and an unarmed woman. You shoot a cop and you will be hunted to extinction."

"Assuming anybody finds out about it."

"That's a fair assumption considering the phone call we made from the office. Before the office went into orbit."

The Ukrainian snorted a laugh. "Is that the best you can come up with?"

Grant sidled another half step to his left. Closer to the workbench. Time was almost up. The bullets must be glowing by now. He jerked his head towards the stairs.

"The armed response units have been surrounding the house for the last ten minutes. Standard police tactics. Deploy and engage. Not with teargas and baton rounds. There's four dead people at the diner. This'll be full breach and the use of deadly force."

He flexed his fingers. Two of the gunmen couldn't help but glance at the bottom of the stairs.

"That count of ten isn't gonna help you now."

There was a sizzle and a pop overhead. Then another. The other four gunmen looked at the ceiling. Grant smiled and shook his head.

"Best thing is you drop your guns and come out with your hands up."

This time the lead Ukrainian did smile. "Like in the movies?"

Grant didn't get a chance to reply. The kitchen windows blew out and gunshots shattered the silence upstairs.

Everything happened real quick after that. The crackle of gunfire in the kitchen drew everyone's attention. Three of the gunmen broke ranks and dashed towards the narrow staircase. The other three swung their guns towards the greatest threat. The ceiling. A knee-jerk reaction that bought Grant a few seconds.

The lead Ukrainian couldn't resist the pull of the gunfire. His face was a picture of comical indecision. He knew he shouldn't be drawn in, but instincts take over in combat situations. The full breach upstairs was a combat situation. It was like tossing a ball at someone. You can't help but try and catch it. The Ukrainian's reflexes were good, but he couldn't override the global reaction. He tried to catch the ball. His gun swung towards the staircase.

The few seconds ticked by in an instant.

Grant snatched the gun from the workbench and swung it in a short arc across the room. He shot the leader as the gun traversed to the three remaining gunmen. The bullet caught him high in the shoulder and spun him around. The spasm shocked his fingers open. He dropped his gun as he was knocked backwards against the Mercedes.

Grant's next two shots hit dead center. Middle of the chest of the first two gunmen his gunsight rested on. They were blasted backwards in a spray of blood. Hope swung his knee against the back of the third gunman's leg, just behind the knee. The gunman's joint buckled and he dropped to the floor. Rivers kicked the gun out of his hand and stamped on his balls. Hope pushed the button as Grant darted for the garage door.

The motor kicked in.

The door began to slide up onto the ceiling track.

"Out."

His shout was unnecessary. Hope was already dropping to a crouch and rolling beneath the half-open door. Rivers hesitated but began to do the same. Grant stepped over the two dead gunmen and picked up their fallen weapons. The third gun had skittered across the floor. He ignored it, pressed the close button, and ducked under the door as the motor switched into reverse.

The snowfall was a moving white curtain across the night. He could barely see beyond his reach but caught movement on his right. Hope had scrambled up the steep embankment at the side of the entrance ramp. His feet slipped in the deepening snow. Grant was halfway up the embankment before he realized that Rivers was wearing indoor shoes. Sensible waitress shoes. Their grips had been worn smooth after months of waiting tables at the diner. She got two steps up the slope before her feet slid back to the bottom.

Grant and Hope reacted in unison. They both reached down with one hand to help pull Rivers up the hill. They both almost caught her outstretched hand as the garage door slid past the half-closed point.

A bloody arm snapped through the closing gap. Strong fingers grabbed Rivers' ankle and yanked her off-balance. She fell and was immediately dragged back under the garage door. The wounded Ukrainian's other hand flicked out, holding the discarded gun. He fired blindly up the embankment. Grant and Hope dived for cover beyond the ridge. The garage door closed all the way to the ground. With Wendy Rivers inside.

05:05 HOURS

GRANT TURNED TO CHARGE back down the embankment, but Hope blocked his way. The eighteen-year-old probationary constable seemed to be bigger and stronger than he'd been before. More mature and level-headed than in the patrol car on Edgebank Close a few short hours ago. Grant tried to barge past him, but Hope slammed a restraining hand against his chest.

"No. You'll just play into his hands."

"We can't leave her."

"We won't leave her. Just have to be later, that's all."

Grant stepped back from the brink. The hand on his chest relaxed. He locked eyes with his protégé and nodded his approval. "Well. When did you grow up and get hair on your balls?"

"When you said this was my first patrol out of company. Single-crewed."

Grant threw a glance at the garage door. It was closed and dark and deadly. Going back through that door would invite a shitstorm of lead and certain death for one captive waitress. Discretion was the better part of valor.

"Good call. But you're double-crewed again now."

He turned his eyes skyward. The snow was blinding. That was both good and bad. Good because it would hide their movement around the house. Bad because it would hide the enemy's movements too. It was also bad because the temperature had dropped like a stone, and Hope only had a thin civvy jacket over his uniform shirt. Grant was wearing a stolen orange windcheater. Not exactly winter clothing.

"Let's get out of this shit."

He struck out along the bottom of the ridge that supported the back garden. The embankment sheltered them from the security lights but more importantly provided a point of reference in the whiteout. Towards the three parked trucks. Grant set off in a loping run that kept his feet from slipping and his body upright. Like cross-country skiing without the skis. Hope fell in step behind him.

The curtain of snow stung Grant's eyes. He squinted into the darkness and turned left away from the embankment towards the turning circle. There was no trail of footprints to follow. His tracks from before were completely obliterated. Silence enveloped them. The gunshots from the house had died down; the shells in the frying pan spent. There was no returning gunfire. The Ukrainians who had charged up the stairs would be securing the kitchen and realizing there was no full breach. Whether they realized they'd been frying panned depended on what damage the bullets had caused.

Distraction technique. It was the best way to buy a little time and focus your enemy's attention in the wrong direction. The trucks loomed out of the darkness, their solid bulk forming behind the constantly shifting snowfall. Distraction. It was what Grant needed now. He felt for the truck key in his pocket. But first they needed to get out of the snow.

THE CANVAS SLAPPED SHUT and Grant tied it as best he could from inside the cargo bed. They were suddenly cocooned in a world of stillness after the constant movement outside. They were also confined in a world of darkness. The back of the truck was pitch black. Even closing his eyes for a count of five only lifted the gloom a single notch. Hope was just a shadowy figure in the dark, hardly there at all. That was no problem for Grant. Night exercises in the army had taught him to use all his senses. Working in the dark was just a different way of working.

"Close your eyes."

Hope sounded bemused. "What?"

"Close your eyes. Count to five. Then open them again."

Grant listened to Hope muttering the count. There was a pause. "Better but not great."

"In the land of the blind, the one-eyed man is king."

"Your point is?"

"For now you don't need to see. Just listen."

They fell into silence. A gentle breeze buffeted the canvas. The snowfall did its thing and muted the night. The cargo bed creaked and groaned. After a few seconds Hope gave up. "Listen to what?"

"Listen to me, fuckwit. There's things we need to get straight."

"Sorry."

Grant sat with his back to the wall. The load bed was empty of cargo but not completely empty. He'd used the limited light from the house to glance around the interior before dropping the tailgate. Trucks this size didn't run on fumes. Their tanks needed gallons of fuel, and if you were distributing illegal narcotics you don't want to be caught short. There were two five-gallon jerry cans strapped to the rear of the cab. Distraction technique. Grant's favorite tactic.

"I don't know when, but any time now half the police force is going to come charging round the corner."

He took the truck key out of his pocket. It sparkled in the gloom. He noticed Hope's eyes follow the key.

"Told you your eyes would adjust."

"You told me that in the land of the blind, the one-eyed man is king."

"Well, now you're the one-eyed man."

He held the key up. "We're gonna need to distract the Ukrainians so I can get Rivers out." He nodded towards the service road. "And we're gonna need somebody to guide the cavalry in."

"That'd be me again. Right?"

"Right."

Hope shuffled on the floorboards. "They killed the chef."

"They did."

His discomfort had nothing to do with the hard floor. Grant could sense Hope's indecision but was encouraged when the probationer said what was on his mind.

"They might have killed the waitress too. By now."

Grant shook his head even though he was just a dark shape in the greater darkness. A reflex.

"Before we got away, maybe. Not now."

A sudden gust of wind buffeted the truck.

"Now they need a hostage. If only to slow my hand."

"Will it slow your hand?"

Grant kept his voice calm even though he felt anything but calm.

"Not if I have to take the shot."

There was a moment's silence, then Hope proved he was still thinking clearly.

"It's going to be hard for them to see a distraction out here."

"On a dark and snowy night? Maybe. What'll make it easier for them to see, d'you think?"

Hope barely needed to think. "Light?"

"That's right. We're gonna give 'em a great big burning light right up the arse."

Hope nodded at the jerry cans. "Burning canvas?"

"And a big fuck-off truck straight through the garage door."

"Which will ignite the fuel drums for the generator and destroy the shipment."

"That's the plan." He put added weight into his voice. "Then you get the fuck down the hill for when the ARVs arrive."

This time the silence was heavier. What Grant had just described was a suicide mission. Not for Hope but for the veteran cop. There was no denying that Grant going back into the house was a very low-percentage move. His chances of saving the girl and getting out alive were slim to nonexistent. There was a feeling of saying goodbye. Grant emphasized his point.

"I want you out of here. Your training is complete."

Hope laughed but without humor. "You sound like Yoda."

"Fuck *Star Trek*."

"*Star Wars*."

Grant leaned forward.

"Right now you're Luke Skywalker and I'm Captain Kirk. And this is my last order: crash the truck and beam the fuck out of here."

05:15 HOURS

THE JERRY CAN LID was stiff. Grant's fingers were cold. It took all his strength to coax them into a firm grip and release the spring-loaded catch. The smell of diesel filled the cargo bed. Hope unfastened the other can and lifted it in both hands to splash diesel over the front of the interior.

Grant barked a harsh whisper. "Better just dowse the back end. You don't want to torch the cab."

Hope sounded embarrassed. "Sorry. Haven't delivered a burning light up the arse before."

The wind outside was getting stronger. It buffeted the truck and flapped the canvas along both sides. Grant untied the rear cover and flicked it open. A gust of wind blew it shut but not before Grant caught sight of the blizzard raging outside. Swirling white demons filled the night. He hefted the jerry can and started sloshing diesel against the right-hand canvas.

"High to low. Let gravity do the work."

Hope did the same on the left.

They were both careful not to splash themselves. Sending a flaming torch didn't need to include burning trousers. The diesel soaked into the canvas and pooled across the cargo bed. Grant half-emptied his can, then stood it against the drop-down tailgate.

"That's enough for now."

Hope did the same. Grant held the canvas flap open. "Over you go."

Hope climbed over the tailgate and dropped to the ground. His feet sank into eight inches of snow. Grant climbed over and stood on the bottom rung of the ladder. He reached in and pushed the first jerry can over. Diesel spewed across the floor. He pushed the second can over too. The fumes were overwhelming. He dropped to the ground next to Hope.

The probationer squinted into the blizzard.

"What about the other trucks?"

Grant shook his head. The orange windcheater stood out in the dark. The guns he'd collected in the garage weighed down the pockets on either side. His first gun was tucked securely down the back of his trousers.

"One'll be enough. We do this right, there won't be anything for 'em to deliver anyway."

He handed the key to Hope, then took Mickey Frevert's lighter out of his pocket. It glinted silver light from the house. Hope held the key up and pointed towards the front of the truck.

"I'd better make sure the engine starts before you torch the back."

Grant followed him round to the driver's door. "I'll put that in your final report. Uses initiative."

Hope stopped with one hand on the door handle. "This won't be the final report. We're going to get out of this."

"I'll put that down too. Optimistic."

Hope looked at the key and then at Grant. "I've just had a thought."

He held the key up. "After soaking the back. What if this is the wrong truck?"

Grant shook his head and turned the key over in Hope's hand. There was a large number 3 painted with Tipp-Ex on the fob. He pointed to the arch of the mudguard above the stepping plate. There was a large white number 3 painted on the dull green metal.

"Have to mark you down for that one."

The wind whipped at the collar of his jacket. The gusts were getting stronger, rumbling out of the night sky like intermittent thunder. Snow swirled all around. He wasn't worried about showing the interior light this time. He released the fob to let Hope open the door.

The rumbling noise wasn't the wind.

It wasn't thunder either.

The short hairs up the back of his neck stood out. He tried to gauge what direction the noise was coming from because he had a pretty good idea what it was. He was surprised if that was the case. In this weather he didn't think they'd scramble X-Ray Nine-Nine.

The thumping helicopter blades grew louder. The noise overrode the sound of the wind. A distant light showed across the ridge to the north. It became a brilliant white beacon, low in the sky and turning the treetops into dancing silhouettes. The searchlight beam split into two and the rolling thunder doubled.

Two helicopters.

Had they scrambled the air ambulance as well? The emergency services acting in concert for once? Grant put a restraining hand on Hope's arm. He squinted into the blizzard towards the oncoming helicopters, then glanced down the service road towards the diner. If the police helicopter was supporting the operation, then the ARVs should be coming across the car park off the A57. He couldn't see any headlights coming this way.

Hope looked at the spotlights cutting a path through the snow-filled sky. "Backup arriving?"

Grant stepped back from the truck for a better view. "I hope so."

He shielded his eyes from the snow with a raised hand. The throbbing beat filled the night. It shook the ground and drowned the beat of his heart. The light was blinding, lighting the entire horizon to the north. The helicopters were invisible behind the spotlights. The wall of light splintered and became two. One chopper drifted towards the turnaround behind the parked trucks. The other went straight for the house. It hovered over the rear garden.

The wind swung the chopper sideways and the security light picked out the lettering along its flank. Grant pulled Hope down into a crouch behind the truck. It wasn't X-Ray Nine-Nine. It wasn't the police or the air ambulance or Pussy Galore's Flying Circus. This was something else.

05:25 HOURS

FOUR ROPES DROPPED FROM the side doors. Four armed men abseiled down to the garden. They dropped fast and hit the ground running. Without pausing to secure the landing zone, they opened fire on the house. Single shots. Rapid fire. Targeting the ground floor windows to keep the defenders' heads down.

The other helicopter lowered itself slowly to the ground in the space behind the trucks. It hovered three feet above the snow and the side doors slid open. Another four men jumped down and immediately dashed across the turnaround towards the ridge. The front two opened fire at the windows on the garage side while the other two deployed towards the ramp. All the ground floor windows on the north and west walls were blown in.

The second helicopter landed in the turnaround and the rotors slowed as the engine was cut. The first helicopter settled on the raised garden above the snowy ridge. The heavy thudding of the blades became a rhythmic whine as they lost momentum.

Grant tugged at Hope's sleeve. He flattened himself to the ground and rolled under the truck. Hope followed Grant's lead.

They watched from just behind the front wheel passenger side. The assault didn't move with military precision, but it was pretty impressive. Voices called out in the dark as the attackers coordinated their approach. A foreign language that was less guttural than the Ukrainians' accent. A South American flavor, maybe Spanish. It seemed completely incongruous in the Yorkshire hills—as if Grant had walked into the middle of some Hollywood movie about drug cartels and international gangsters. He watched and listened and assessed the visitors' expertise and weaponry.

The first group approached the house from the garden level. They spread out across the snow, guns raised. Two had some kind of assault rifle, and the other two had heavy-duty handguns. The initial barrage of shots had taken out the ground floor windows. There had been no return fire from the house. The rifles tracked the bedroom windows as they neared the house, while the handguns focused on the kitchen.

There was movement in a window on the top left. A curtain twitched, then the glass was broken from inside. Two shots rang out, the muzzle flash illuminating the frame and sill. Both rifles swung up and left. Three shots each in quick succession. A good spread. Accurate. The gunman in the window was blasted backwards into the darkened room. The rifles scanned the rest of the first floor windows. Clear.

The second group had swarmed past the garage ramp. Two rifles and two handguns. This time the rifles hung back at the top of the ramp to cover the handguns as they approached the side wall. The only window on the ground floor was the toilet with the louver slats that Grant had removed to climb through. There was a landing window above it. The rifles covered the landing. One handgun concentrated on the toilet window. His colleague covered the garage door.

No more shots were fired. The initial barrage had either broken the will of the defenders or shot, wounded, or killed them all. Grant reckoned it was the former. The opening salvos had been about shock and awe instead of targeted firing. There might have been some casualties inside, but more from stray rounds and ricochets than individual shots.

Swirling snow hung a lace curtain across the scene. It was only the brightness of the security lights that allowed Grant to see what was going on. His angle was low beneath the shelter of the truck, but he saw the first group approach the kitchen door at the same time as the second group rounded the corner to the front door. There was no resistance. There was a crash from the front of the house as the porch door was breached. The kitchen door was kicked open, and all four went inside.

The entire action had taken less than five minutes. The helicopter blades had spun down to nothing. The engines were quiet. After the cacophony of gunfire, the night fell silent again. Deep snow and the swirling blizzard sucked the last echoes out of the battle, and the night settled back into a snowstorm at an all-night truck stop and diner.

Grant blinked and let out a deep breath. Until then he hadn't realized he'd been holding his breath. His heart raced. He felt Hope's stillness beside him and put a reassuring hand on his shoulder. Hope blew out his cheeks as he let out an explosive sigh. Grant could feel the tension humming through Hope's body. Grant hit the pressure-relief button.

"Well, that's fucked plan A."

Hope snorted a laugh, and the tension eased. "I'd say that's fucked everything."

It was hard to argue with that. Any idea of getting away clean after rescuing the maiden from the dragon had been kicked into a cocked hat. The dragon had just been defeated, only to be replaced by a more vicious dragon. The maiden was in even greater peril. Wendy Rivers could be a casualty or even dead. Grant refused to accept that. The last time he'd seen her, she was being dragged under the garage door. That placed her in the basement when the assault took place. None of the gunfire had targeted the basement. She was safe. He had to believe that to justify what he was going to do next.

"It doesn't change the basics."

Hope turned to look at Grant, his face the picture of disbelief. "You're kidding, aren't you?"

Grant shook his head. "She's still in there. Bad guys are still armed. And we still need a diversion."

"A diversion? We need the SAS."

"I was in the SAS."

This time Hope's expression bordered on awe. His jaw dropped open and his eyes grew wide. The teenage probationer looked like he'd just met Elvis, except he was probably too young to remember Elvis. The snow continued to drift out of the night sky. The gusting wind formed it into swirls and eddies.

"The SAS?"

Grant met Hope's questioning look with a level gaze. "Not exactly. Kind of a subsidiary."

Hope let out a breath that was all steam. "I thought you said you were a typist."

Grant smiled. "I did some typing. Point is, I know what to do next."

Hope let the weight of those words sink in for a moment. He scanned the snowscape and the blizzard and the house. He glanced towards the helicopter sitting like a squat bug behind the parked trucks. When he turned back to Grant, his face asked the question but he kept quiet.

Grant held him with steady eyes and lowered his voice.

"It's just gonna be a bit more dangerous than before."

05:40 HOURS

Ten minutes later Grant disappeared into the blizzard, keeping out of the brilliant white halo surrounding the house. The security lights were a necessary evil. In an ideal world he would have shot out the bulbs and plunged the exterior into darkness, but seeing what the invaders were doing was just as important as them not seeing him. He paused in the shadows and scanned the house again.

Things hadn't changed since his final evaluation from under the truck. The lights had gone on upstairs, but the activity was limited to a quick search and rounding up any strays. He'd seen that through the windows. There appeared to be just one extra man, apart from the one who'd been shot, posted in the bedroom, and he was herded down to join his colleagues. Most of the other activity was in the kitchen and hallway. The rest was hidden from view in the basement garage. Grant paid particular attention to the comings and goings through the wood-panelled door beneath the main staircase.

Looking at the house from a different angle gave him a view of the front. It confirmed what he'd seen from the truck.

The upper floor had been secured, then vacated. Any threats from up there had been neutralized. Any threats from outside would come at ground level. The goods the intruders had come to acquire were in the subbasement. They weren't expecting any more trouble from the bedrooms. The bedrooms were empty. So that was where Grant was going to force entry.

He glanced over his shoulder towards the turnaround. The three square shapes were barely visible through the snow. The helicopter beyond them was just a distant shadow. Grant checked his watch. 5:40 AM. Timing was going to be a problem. Once he was inside there was no way for him to signal Hope, so they'd synchronized watches and agreed on a time. Six o'clock. If Grant hadn't secured Rivers by then, he was in deep shit anyway.

The diversion would be massive. Bigger than a few bullets in a frying pan. More destructive than a few broken windows. Big enough to guide the ARVs in even without Hope's help. Because Grant was about to do what he'd spent six months telling his probationer not to do. Go charging in waving his warrant card without a radio or backup. He hoped the enemy would cease and desist, otherwise he'd simply have to shoot them.

Grant crossed the snow in a crouch, keeping close to the tree line that ended six feet from the front porch. The door hung at an angle from its damaged hinges, but it was the window above it that concerned him. The one he'd climbed out of nearly three hours ago.

The one with the broken lock.

GRANT SLID THE WINDOW closed and resisted the urge to tap the snow off his shoes. The bedroom hadn't changed. The double bed was still against the back wall, and the en suite bathroom was still a gaping black rectangle with the door open and the lights off. A thin line of yellow light showed under the landing door. The room was as quiet as the grave. Even his breath and heartbeat were dimmed to silence.

He crossed the room and put one ear to the door. He could hear voices and movement from downstairs. Nothing violent. Nothing angry. This was the calm that followed the battle, a far deeper stillness than the fabled calm before the storm. If Grant got this right, they'd be one and the same because he was going to bring on a shitstorm.

Not yet, though. First he needed to find Wendy Rivers. She would no doubt be held with the Ukrainian prisoners. Judging by the movement he'd seen through the windows, they weren't being held in the kitchen or living room. The most sensible place to keep your captives secure was in the midst of your own forces. Since most of the enemy personnel were underground, that meant Rivers was either in the garage or the subbasement. A lot of armed men to get through. Almost impossible to survive a one-man assault against superior numbers. A frontal assault would achieve nothing except a few men dead, the rescue aborted, and Wendy Rivers still in custody.

Softly, softly, catchee monkey.

Under circumstances like that, there was only one sure way of getting to the heart of the enemy position, and that wasn't trying to shoot your way through. It was to get invited in. Just like the vampires in all those old Hammer films he used to watch at Moor Grange School for Boys. The only people invited to the inner circle were the ones being held captive in the basement.

Grant prepared to give himself up. He checked that his supplies were in place, then took the gun out of his pocket. He released the magazine to make sure it was the one with the most shots fired, then rammed it back into the base of the grip and dropped the gun back in his pocket. It pulled the orange windcheater down at one side. He patted the crotch of his trousers to make sure the second gun was securely hidden. Even professional police officers tended to avoid groping another fella's wedding tackle during a custody search. He hoped these guys were no different.

He took a deep breath to calm himself.

His heart rate slowed.

Then he opened the bedroom door and stepped out onto the landing.

THE STAIRS DIDN'T CREAK. The carpet muffled his footsteps. Nobody heard him come down the staircase. It was embarrassing. Here he was, trying to surrender, and nobody even realized he was there. He was standing at the bottom of the stairs in a bright orange windcheater with his arms held out like Jesus on the cross, and nobody noticed him.

He'd been right about the enemy activity. It was centered on the wood-panelled door beneath the stairs. One man came up and went into the kitchen. Two men came out of the living room and went down the narrow staircase. Grant heard the kettle switched on and the clink of teaspoons in cups. Somebody was making a bunch of hot drinks. If the pecking order was the same for drug dealers as everywhere else, then the person making the drinks was at the bottom. Like the office tea boy or the new probationer on the shift.

The ideal person to accept Grant's surrender.

Better be careful, though. New staff could be the jumpiest. Grant kept his hands away from his sides and walked into the living room.

He glanced at the table. The chair hadn't been moved. The previous owner of the orange windcheater was still under the table flap. That boded well for Grant's plan. These fellas hadn't cleared the room as well as a military assault team would have done. In his army days, whoever missed checking the table would have been canned first day of training.

He crossed the room to the kitchen door. It was open. The tea boy was ladling coffee into six mugs on a serving tray. One side of his heavy winter coat hung lower than the other. Same as Grant's. He could easily sneak up behind him and snap his neck before the gun could be drawn. That wasn't the plan, though. Grant moved slowly. He didn't want to startle the guy into taking a snap shot.

Keeping his arms out and hands open, he stepped through the door.

"You missed one."

The tea boy didn't jump at first. He glanced at the mugs on the tray to see if he'd missed putting coffee in one of them. Grant felt embarrassed for him. Then the penny dropped and he spun round, snatching for his gun.

Grant waved both hands in a calming gesture.

"I come in peace."

Grant expected the gunman to be young and fresh faced but was surprised to see the acne-scarred face of a thirty-year-old. The olive skin and dark eyes of a South American. Somewhere like that. Once the gun was drawn, it was handled expertly. Once the surprise wore off, he seemed confident.

"Where you come from?"

"Originally? Or just now?"

The man's tone didn't change. "Where you come from?"

Grant pointed his right hand at the ceiling. "Front bedroom. In the shower."

The man shouted towards the wood-panelled door in Spanish. Two short bursts, urgency dripping from his voice. A few moments later, the two men who had just gone down came back up again. There was a brief exchange of words, then the gunman waved his spare hand at Grant's coat pocket.

"Take out the gun, my friend."

Grant took the gun out, holding the butt between finger and thumb. One of the others took it, then stepped back. They covered Grant while the tea boy patted him down. A cursory search. Checked Grant's pockets and felt the sides of his body, arms, and legs. Nowhere near his groin. There was nothing to find except his wallet. He flipped it open and saw the West Yorkshire Police warrant card. It wasn't as impressive as an American cop's shield, even a South American cop's shield, but his eyes widened.

"*Policia*?"

The other two stiffened. The tea boy held the warrant card out. "*Policia*?"

Grant nodded but didn't answer. The tea boy got the message. "Why are you here?"

Grant shrugged and kept his tone light. "Because the Ukrainians are criminals, and I've come to arrest them."

The tea boy smiled. "Then you have come a little late."

"So it seems."

The tea boy seemed to ask everything twice. "Why are you here?"

Grant let out a sigh. This was going to be hard work. He lowered his arms and pointed to the wood-panelled door.

"Take me to your leader. I'll explain everything."

The tea boy tilted his head to one side as he considered that. Time was ticking by. Grant couldn't afford to waste too much standing in the kitchen. He was about to say something else when the tea boy nodded the other men towards the basement stairs. He said something in Spanish. Then he spoke in English.

"Go with them. I must finish coffee."

The two men urged Grant forward, and he ducked beneath the wood-panelled door. As he headed down the narrow staircase, he could hear the clink of a teaspoon stirring hot water into the mugs.

05:50 HOURS

THE GARAGE WAS A hive of activity. It had a completely different tempo to the last time he'd been down here. It seemed that tonight Grant was destined to visit everywhere twice. He came out of the narrow door at the bottom of the stairs with his hands held out and a gun in his back. More proof if it were needed that these weren't professionals. Best way to get disarmed is to stand too close and stick a gun in your captive's back.

The two South Americans followed Grant into the garage and told him to stand still. Grant obliged, using the time to catalog the changes since his last visit. He stood with his arms held out like a cross and began with the things that hadn't changed. The barrels of fuel oil were still in the corner. The workbench and metal cupboard were still up against the back wall. The generator still hummed. The grey Mercedes still took up half the floor space.

Those were the constants. Everything else had changed. Instead of a group of armed Ukrainians standing in front of the up-and-over door, there was a gang of swarthy South Americans busily stacking cardboard boxes at the top of the subbasement steps. The bodies of the Ukrainians had gone. Petrol fumes and sweat overpowered the smell of cordite and gunfire. The South Americans were working hard. All except one. An older man with greying temples stood apart from the rest, overseeing the drug seizure. He turned when Grant was nudged forward. Hard eyes examined the latest captive and took in the distinctive orange windcheater and short-cropped hair.

"You are the other driver?"

Grant caught a flicker of orange through the subbasement door. The other two truck drivers, also wearing orange windcheaters. Good. That meant Wendy Rivers must be down there with the other prisoners. The man repeated the question.

"Are you the other truck driver?"

Before Grant could answer, he heard the clinking of cups on a tray behind him.

"He's a cop. I caught him sneaking through the kitchen."

An exaggeration that told Grant something else about these people—or at least one of them. The tea boy was keen to impress. Judging by the look on the older man's face, it wasn't working.

"Did you search him?"

The tea boy grunted something at the man behind Grant. The man held Grant's gun up for inspection by the butt. The older man came over and took the gun. He nodded at the second man.

"Search him again."

The tea boy looked crestfallen. He wasn't trusted and that seemed to hurt. He walked around Grant and placed the tea tray on the workbench, then watched as the second man began a more thorough search. Starting at the top, then working down. Using both hands in concert, he felt along Grant's left arm from wrist to shoulder. He did the same with the right. He scrunched up the windcheater's collar, then ran his hands down both sides of Grant's body. He felt Grant's back from shoulder blades to waist. He did the same with the front.

Nothing.

The man dropped to a crouch and started on Grant's legs. Same procedure as with the arms. Both hands together running up either side of each leg. From ankle to thigh. Left leg first. Then the right.

Nothing.

Grant felt a wave of relief when the man stood up. It was short lived. The man felt Grant's buttocks, pinching the back pockets of his trousers. Finally he showed no embarrassment as he squeezed Grant's groin and stopped. He tapped the hard metal hiding down the front of Grant's trousers. Glanced over his shoulder at the older man, who gave a curt nod.

The man didn't ask Grant to hand the gun over. He tugged Grant's belt out and shoved his hand down the gap. He came up with the second gun and stepped back. The older man took it from him.

"You two—back upstairs. We don't want any more surprises."

The tea boy looked shamefaced and watched the other two leave.

The older man ignored him, concentrating on Grant, still standing with his arms out like Jesus on the cross. The man waved for Grant to lower his arms.

"My nephew. We all have our crosses to bear."

The rest of the South Americans continued to bring the boxes up from the subbasement. The older man put both guns on the workbench next to the steaming mugs of coffee before turning back to Grant.

"Now tell me what you are doing here."

Grant gave the short version. The one that said the Ukrainians were bad people and police officers were supposed to arrest bad people. Basically what he'd told the nephew. The reason he gave the short version was because time was running out. It was five to six in the morning. This time of year dawn wouldn't begin to feather the horizon until half past seven at the earliest. With the pregnant snow clouds, maybe quarter to eight. Dawn wasn't the issue. Jamie Hope was.

Grant looked down at his hands before speaking. Ruffled the sleeve of his windbreaker so he could take a sneaky peak at his watch. Four minutes to go. The plan sped through his head, and Grant could see Hope in his mind's eye preparing to execute it.

Hope finished dowsing the cargo beds of the last two trucks. He soaked the strips of cloth and tamped them down into the fuel tanks of both trucks. The snow was easing, becoming less of a blizzard and more like a gentle snowstorm. The flakes were smaller too.

He took the box of matches he'd found in the cab before Grant left and checked he still had the key for the first truck. He'd asked for the lighter but Grant needed that himself. If everything went according to plan. Hope concentrated on the part he had control over. Just one of the things that Grant had taught him during the six months he'd been Hope's training officer.

He checked his watch. Almost time.

"And you came all the way here to arrest the Ukrainians?"

The man with the grey temples seemed to be amused. His eyes lost some of their hardness and there was a jovial lilt to his voice. Grant could see him turning over the evidence in his mind.

"I came here for a drink and a chat. The Ukrainians were a happy accident."

Mr. Grey tilted his head.

"Not so happy for the Ukrainians."

"The way it turned out, no. Not for them."

Mr. Grey looked Grant up and down. "You do not dress like a policeman."

Grant opened the orange jacket to show his uniform shirt. "I'm off-duty."

"Yet you were going to arrest a group of armed drug dealers single handed."

"I've called for backup. Should be here any minute now."

Mr. Grey smiled. "Ah, the fabled reinforcements. Like in the movies when the guy says he's put everything in a letter and it will be posted to the news if anything happens to him."

"Nothing like that. I called them from the office."

Grant made a show of checking his watch.

Three minutes to go.

He locked eyes with Mr. Grey. "Snow must be holding 'em up. So I could give you a head start if you get going now."

Mr. Grey's eyes grew hard again. "Count to ten? Like you told the Ukrainians?"

Grant felt a shiver run down his spine. He tried to remember if any of the Ukrainians who'd heard Grant give the warning had survived. A short man with broad shoulders brought the last box up from the subbasement and set it on top of the pile. He spoke to Mr. Grey in rapid-fire Spanish. The only thing Grant could pick out was "Señor Dominguez." Dominguez threw an angry look at the stocky man, and the man's face drained of color. The nephew tried to diffuse the situation by handing mugs of coffee around. Dominguez waved him away and turned his attention back to Grant.

"I believe you when you say you wanted to arrest the Ukrainians."

He took a step towards the captured policeman.

"But the Ukrainians are history."

His eyes held Grant's in a hypnotic stare.

"So I'll rephrase the question. What are you doing coming back here? It is not so you can arrest a bunch of Ukrainian drug manufacturers."

The nephew took a sip of coffee and watched. The short man with the broad shoulders straightened the boxes. Two more men shut the subbasement door and came up the steps to help.

Grant took a deep breath.

Dominguez's eyes hardened. "Why did you come back?"

Grant let the breath out slowly through his nose. "Well, there is one thing."

He nodded at the subbasement door.

"Not everyone you've got locked up down there is a Ukrainian drug dealer."

He relaxed his knees and flexed his shoulders.

"And part of a policeman's job is to protect innocent bystanders."

Dominguez's eyes crinkled into a smile that didn't touch his lips. Footsteps sounded on the narrow staircase coming down from the house. Grant focused on the man with greying temples. Dominguez shook his head.

"There are no innocent bystanders here."

The footsteps weren't heavy, but Grant didn't notice that.

"There is one. The waitress that worked at the diner."

Dominguez stopped shaking his head and broke out a sad little smile. "You have come to rescue the woman. I commend you for that."

The footsteps reached the bottom of the stairs.

"But you proceed under a false assumption."

Dominguez leaned his head forward and repeated himself. "There are no innocent bystanders here."

The footsteps came into the garage behind Grant. Not heavy footsteps. Female footsteps. Grant looked over his shoulder as Wendy Rivers crossed to stand beside Dominguez. Dominguez's smile turned into a grin.

"How do you think we kept an eye on this operation in the first place?"

05:58 HOURS

GRANT FELT THE AIR suck out of his lungs, but he didn't let the surprise show on his face. This changed everything. He tried to think back to the first time he'd met the woman who became his midnight confidant. How long ago had that been? How long had she worked as the nightshift waitress? He couldn't remember. Three months? Five? Six at a push. He'd already been a long-term customer by then, he knew that for sure. He looked at her and smiled.

Rivers couldn't meet his gaze.

Grant nodded at the mugs of coffee on the workbench. "I'd've thought they'd have you make the coffee instead of Mini Dominguez over there."

His tone hardened.

"I guess some rivers run deeper than others."

Rivers looked into his eyes and forced herself not to blink. Her expression was blank but there was something behind those eyes that spoke of other things. Shame first, but something darker hid behind it. Fear.

Grant understood. She had plenty to be afraid of. More people were going to die here tonight, and Dominguez wasn't going to leave any witnesses. That meant goodbye Jim Grant and almost certainly farewell Wendy Rivers.

"I never saw you as coming from south of the border. But then again my American geography isn't that great."

Dominguez feigned sadness. "Aw. We've hurt your feelings. It wouldn't be a surprise if you'd seen her name written down."

Grant glanced at her plastic name badge. It only had her first name.

Dominguez caught the look and explained.

"It is Rivas. Spelled R-I-V-A-S. Not Rivers."

Grant split his attention between the waitress and the drug dealer. "Maybe it should be Windy instead of Wendy. Spelled W-I-N-D-Y. More winding twists than a snake in the grass."

Dominguez moved closer to Rivas. "That is very poetic but rather bitter. I did not think you were a bitter man."

"I prefer bitter over mild. Tetley's Bitter is the northerner's drink."

"A witty Bitter drinker. I will comment on that when I see my brother."

"Another Dominguez? What's his name? So I can tell you apart when I come and arrest you."

"I think you already know too much, my friend."

Grant watched Dominguez step beside Rivas and knew what was coming. He shifted his weight from the left leg to the right, feeling the cold hard metal of the third gun against his groin. The one that had been hidden behind the second gun during the search.

Dominguez grabbed Rivas' arm.

"And so do you, my dear."

The second box-stacker grabbed Rivas's other arm and pulled her backwards. She staggered against the pile of boxes, shock flaring her nostrils. The fear that had been hidden behind her deadpan expression flashed across her face. Dominguez let go of her arm. The box-stacker jerked a thumb at the subbasement door and grunted a question. "With the others?"

Dominguez appeared to consider the question, and the smooth charm vanished from his face. A lustful glint flickered behind his eyes. A cruel smile played across his lips as he shook his head.

"Take her to the bedroom."

That wasn't good. Things weren't going according to plan. Grant watched Dominguez follow her up the narrow staircase, but his mind's eye was seeing Jamie Hope. The young probationer should be ready to set his part in motion as the minutes ticked towards six o'clock. That wasn't going according to plan either.

Hope checked his watch for the last time. Almost zero six hundred hours. The blizzard had nearly stopped. That was good and bad. At least the snow wouldn't get any deeper, but it meant the curtain of drifting flakes made him easier to see. He took a match out of the box and glanced over his shoulder.

The nearest helicopter was clearly visible. Light from the house reflected off the curved body and domed windscreen. The pilot sat patiently at the controls, waiting for the assault team to return or for instructions to be received. Hope wondered if he was in touch with the house.

That's when Hope decided to change the plan. He couldn't risk the pilot seeing what the young constable was doing in the clearing skies and reporting back to the men in the house. Grant needed a diversion, not a clear report from outside.

The decision didn't change the order of the plan, only the direction of his getaway. He walked around the front of the truck on the blindside from the helicopter and went to the farthest diesel-soaked rag. The match rasped in the silence. He touched the flame to the rag and it bloomed into blue, bright light. The blue changed to yellow as the rag caught fire. Hope quickly crossed to the middle truck and lit the second rag.

The flames stood out in the dark. There was no time to waste. Hope went to the open flap at the back of the truck marked number 3. The one he had the keys for. The cargo bed stunk of diesel. He took a handful of matches and wedged them into the end of the box. He struck a match and set them alight. The matchbox flared to life, and he dropped it through the open canvas. Blue and yellow flames spread across the cargo bed and crawled up the canvas sides.

He glanced at the helicopter. There was movement in the cockpit.

Hope jumped into the cab and started the truck. The engine roared at the first attempt. He looked at the brightly lit house and the ramp leading to the garage. The three air vents poking out of the snow. Plan A had been to drive the truck into the garage and set the fuel drums alight. Plan B had changed at Grant's suggestion. Drive the flaming truck down the access road to the diner and draw the attackers' fire away from the house.

Hope was improvising Plan C.

He gunned the engine to make sure it wasn't going to stall. He threw one final look at the security lights blazing across the house, then focused on the rear-view mirrors. The helicopter glinted in the wash from the security lights.

Hope engaged reverse gear and slipped the clutch. Instead of driving down the hill, he feathered the clutch until the big, heavy wheels gripped the snow. The truck rolled backwards, slowly at first but then building momentum once the wheels dug themselves out of the drifting snow.

The helicopter didn't stand a chance. Deadweight and solid metal slammed into the cockpit at thirty miles an hour. The blazing cargo bed destroyed the smooth fiberglass shell. The remaining jerry cans were knocked over and spilled more diesel onto the inferno. Then the first truck exploded in the distance. A huge fireball bloomed into the night sky. The second truck followed almost immediately. The truck beds and fuel tanks were ripped apart.

Hope was out and running before the third truck did the same, blasting hot metal into the ruptured helicopter fuel tank. The double explosion filled the night with broiling flames. Hope didn't look back as he charged towards the house. Unarmed and alone. No radio and no backup. Just his warrant card and a willing heart. It wasn't going to be enough.

06:00 HOURS

THE FIRST EXPLOSION SHOOK the basement. Dust and plaster dropped from the ceiling. Grant was halfway down the worn stone steps to the subbasement door, being shoved into captivity by the two remaining South Americans. Dominguez had ordered him locked away as he went upstairs with Rivas. Grant couldn't afford to think about that. He needed to remain focused on what he could control. What he could control was tucked down the front of his trousers.

Then the explosion thumped outside. Followed by a second and a third.

That third one was worrying. Hope should have been halfway down the hill to guide the ARVs in when they arrived. Truck number 3 shouldn't have exploded yet. They'd set the diesel at the rear of the cargo bed. It should just be a flaming torch drawing attention away from the house.

The explosions did draw the attention of the South Americans. The first one had just slid open the bolt on the door. The second was standing behind Grant. Both turned their heads towards the noise outside. That was all the time Grant needed.

The gun didn't come out in a smooth, quick draw, but it came out fast enough. Grant shot the man in front of him, then spun to shoot the second man at the top of the steps. Only one of them was armed. Grant picked up the fallen gun from the stairwell and pushed the subbasement door open.

The dead Ukrainians were stacked beneath a tarpaulin against the wall. Grant didn't stop to count the feet sticking out of one end. He concentrated on the four standing behind the long table that ran the length of the cellar. There was an array of complicated equipment on the table. A manufacturing process that Grant didn't even pretend to understand. Apart from a dusting of white powder, the table was clean. This wasn't the kind of industry that tolerated waste. Everything the Ukrainians made was neatly packaged and stored in the boxes at the top of the steps.

Grant had to make a split-second decision: cut and run or stay and fight. If he was going to stay, it was for one reason only, and she was being held in the first floor bedroom. Between here and there was an army of South Americans who would all be on their guard after the explosions outside. Explosions that were supposed to act as a decoy while Grant rescued the innocent bystander from the cellar.

Except Wendy Rivas wasn't an innocent bystander.

Did that matter?

Split-second decision.

No, it didn't. She may have made a bad choice, but he couldn't leave her to face the consequences. Trouble was, she wasn't close to hand anymore, so getting to her was his first problem.

Another split-second decision.

He needed to divide the South Americans' attention—attack them on two fronts. Keep them busy on the ground floor while he snuck round from behind. He needed a secondary force. Men with good reason to attack the interlopers.

He leaned against the doorframe and looked at the men behind the table.

"Any of you lot speak English?"

The Ukrainians didn't take much persuading. Even in broken English it made more sense for them to attack their captors than to stay down here in the cellar. Grant had a brief moment's pause when he questioned the idea of giving guns to the men who'd killed the chef and intended to kill the waitress, but he brushed his doubts aside. When your back's against the wall, you've got to use what's available. He had no choice.

Grant handed the gun he'd picked up off the steps to the first man who stepped forward. A short man with broad shoulders. The two truck drivers appeared less keen to go on the offensive, but they had no choice either. Grant went up the steps and crossed to the workbench. Steam drifted up from the unused mugs of coffee. The two guns that had been taken from him lay next to the tray. He picked them up and offered them butts first.

The second gunman and one of the truck drivers took them. The gunman checked the chamber was empty and dropped the magazine out of the grip. It was fully loaded. He slammed it back in and worked the slide. The truck driver took his on trust. Speaking in their own language they paired off, a gunman and a truck driver in each group. One pair moved to the bottom of the narrow staircase. The other pair went to the garage door. There was a brief meeting of eyes, then they all nodded.

Grant pushed the green button. The motor hummed and the garage door began to slide open. The two men ducked under the gap and jogged up the ramp. The snow had stopped but the slope was still six inches deep. As soon as they were out, Grant hit the red button. The motor reversed and the door slid down. The other two didn't wait for it to close. They raised their guns and disappeared into the narrow staircase single file.

The garage door clanged shut. The generator pulsed in the corner. Apart from that, the basement was quiet. Grant's breath sounded loud in his ears. He didn't waste time appreciating the peace and quiet. There were things needed doing before he went into action.

First thing was to check the Mercedes. He fished the keys out of his sock and opened the driver's door. Made a quick search of the glove box and only came up with a road map and a torch. No weapons. He turned the ignition. The engine started first time. The petrol gauge showed three quarters full. He turned the engine off and put the keys in his pocket.

Next he took the lighter out of his other sock and flicked it open. Rasped the wheel to spark a light. It still worked. He crossed to the workbench and rummaged through the tools. Selected a large Phillips screwdriver with a pointed end. He jabbed it into the wooden bench to test its strength. It stuck in the scratched surface like a knife.

The fuel drums were ribbed metal but no thicker than any other container. Grant emptied two of the coffee mugs and went to the first drum. He stabbed three holes in the side and filled the mugs from the flow. He splashed the contents over the stacked boxes, then refilled the mugs. He repeated the process until the boxes were soaked before putting the mugs down and stabbing another half-dozen holes in the drum. He did the same with the second drum. Fuel spilled out across the uneven floor. Like all liquids, it found the path of least resistance and began to run down the steps into the subbasement. The smell was strong and made Grant's eyes water. He put the lighter in his pocket. Later, for the inferno.

He looked around the garage. Everything was set. He checked that the leaking fuel wasn't spreading towards the Mercedes. It wasn't. The dip in the floor was keeping it to the opposite side of the room. The scene was set. Now he had to get upstairs and rescue the girl.

The dumbwaiter hatch in the wall was closed. Grant doubted if it had been used in ten years. Probably more. Not since the original owners had lived with ideas above their station. Nobody used dumbwaiters these days. They must have been fans of *Upstairs Downstairs* or maybe had a disabled mother who needed to be served dinner in her bedroom.

Grant opened the hatch and looked inside. All he could see was darkness. That didn't bother him. Darkness was where he was headed.

06:10 HOURS

THE DUMBWAITER HAD SETTLED at the bottom of the shaft. That meant he wouldn't have to risk the noise of ropes and pulleys and squeaky wheels by pulling it out of the way. The shaft was wide and straight. The dumbwaiter was big enough to take a full dinner and accompaniments loaded on a tray.

There was a glimmer of light halfway up. Light from the kitchen spilling through the uneven cracks in the serving hatch. Farther up there was only darkness. Maybe a hint of brightness near the top but not as much light as the kitchen. That would be the front bedroom. With no lights on. That suggested Dominguez had taken Rivas into the master bedroom across the hall.

Grant made sure the gun was tucked firmly in his belt and began to climb. After the confined space of the ventilation channel at the diner, this was like climbing up the M1. Broad and long with no obstructions.

He was halfway up before he heard the first sounds of gunfire.

The Ukrainians were less selective in their targeting than the helicopter assault team. The pair that were skirting the outside of the house only had one gun, but their objective was to draw the fire of the South Americans inside. They climbed the snowy bank towards the kitchen, the driver throwing a wary glance over his shoulder at the three blazing trucks and the charred wreckage of the helicopter.

The gunman focused on the kitchen windows. There was hardly any glass left in them. Shadowy figures moved around inside. The Ukrainians were standing in bright light against a white background. They needed to even the odds. The gunman took careful aim and shot out the security lights. Then he blasted away through the kitchen windows. He didn't see the scurrying figure dart around the back of the conservatory in the freshly minted dark.

Jamie Hope hadn't been in a gunfight before. He'd never even handled a gun apart from the air rifles at the fair. He was unarmed but single minded. One way or another, he was getting inside that house to help his tutor. When the security lights went out, he saw his chance. A branching network of drainpipes, waste pipes, and toilet overflow pipes ran up the side of the house behind the conservatory. The main pipe split into three on the first floor. The bathroom and toilet. The best window to climb in through. He doubted anyone would be using the toilet during a gunfight.

When the firing started, he skirted the conservatory and began to climb.

The gunshots sounded loud in the relative quiet of the dumbwaiter shaft. A few distant blasts from outside followed by a fusillade of returned fire from the kitchen as Grant climbed past the serving hatch. His only danger was from ricochets or being caught in the crossfire.

He quickly scrambled up beyond the hatch and headed towards the bedroom. The tempo of gunfire became more irregular and spaced out. An occasional burst from the kitchen. A couple of shots from outside. Then a fresh salvo from somewhere deep inside the house. The narrow staircase leading up from the garage. The pincer movement as the Ukrainians caught the South Americans between two forces.

Grant reached the first floor without incident. He braced his shoulders against the sides of the shaft and wedged his feet into the grooves and cross members. His head was level with the serving hatch. He listened for sounds of movement in the bedroom. There were none. There were no voices and no gunshots. All the action was downstairs or on the landing.

He slid the hatch open and peered into the gloom.

The bedroom was empty; the only light was that filtering in through the tinted window above the landing door. He hauled himself up and folded his body through the hatch, rolling onto the floor beside the bed. He waited in a crouch to see if anyone had heard him. His mind raced, visualizing the first floor layout. The landing across the top of the stairs. First floor bathroom and toilet at the rear of the house. Another room next to that. The master bedroom across the hallway and the front bedroom where he was hiding.

His eyes picked out something he hadn't noticed before.

There was another door in the far corner against the interior wall. The two main bedrooms were adjoining rooms, like in a posh hotel. He wouldn't have to cross the firing range that the landing was about to become. He could sneak in the back door. If it wasn't locked.

The pincer movement worked. The weight of shot was forcing the South Americans back even though they boasted superior numbers. The two Ukrainians from the garage staircase breached the hallway at the same time as the two from outside clambered through the glassless kitchen windows.

The South Americans laid down covering fire as they retreated up the main stairs. The unarmed truck driver took one in the shoulder and roared with pain. Blood turned his orange windcheater dark red from the top right all the way across his chest. He tried to stem the flow with a tea towel but the bullet had obviously hit something serious. He slid down the wall and sat staring into space as he bled out.

His comrade barely gave him a second glance as he cut across the living room to the other door. The new angle gave him a better line of fire. The two from the garage moved out from the wood-panelled door. All three shot out the wooden banister rails, sending splinters and ricochets flying across the stairs.

The defenders were forced back.

Smoke drifted across the staircase.

The battle was about to shift to the first floor landing.

Jamie Hope clambered through the bathroom window and narrowly avoided falling down the toilet. The lid was up, but at least it had been flushed. He reached out and closed the lid but still had to climb in headfirst. His legs twisted through the window behind him and knocked the shelf above the sink. An empty glass tumbled into the bath with a crash.

Hope froze with one leg on the ground. The breaking glass echoed off the tiled walls.

He held his breath, half expecting the door to burst open. Nobody came in. There was too much noise coming from the stairs and hallway. He set his other leg on the ground and flexed his neck. The bones cracked, but he felt better. Grant's words ran through Hope's head. *Don't go wading in without communication or backup. Off-duty is off-duty.*

Hope had never felt more off-duty and he had never been farther from communication and backup. This wasn't the time to go waving his warrant card. These fellas weren't going to cease and desist. But Grant had taught him something else. Always back your colleagues. With that thought in mind, he waited for a lull in proceedings and prepared to enter the fray.

GRANT TURNED THE HANDLE slowly. The door to the adjoining room wasn't locked. He put his ear to the door and listened. He heard a slap and a scream followed by racking sobs. An angry voice with a heavy accent. Dominguez. The sobs grew quieter, then were replaced with a sniffling nose and a cough. There were no more sounds of violence.

Grant opened the door a crack, a fraction of an inch at a time. He didn't want to make any jarring movements that could draw attention from inside. The movement was so slow it was almost invisible. The door opened inwards. A stroke of good luck. He only had to open a big enough gap to put one eye to. The angle gave him a truncated view. He scanned the room as best he could.

Dominguez stood with his back to the door. He hadn't wasted any time. Rivas was sitting on the edge of the double bed, her torn blouse revealing a bra strap and one heaving breast. She also had a cut and a bruise on her right cheekbone. Fresh blood trickled from the cut.

The waitress had been a punch bag once too often tonight. Grant wasn't going to let it happen again. He drew the gun out of his belt and stepped through the door.

06:20 HOURS

"WHY DON'T YOU TRY that on somebody your own size?"

Dominguez spun round. The oily charm he'd displayed in the underground garage had been replaced by a slithering evil that burned from his eyes and twisted his smile into an ugly slash with lips. One hand dripped blood where he'd struck Rivas across the face. Lee Adkins all over again.

Rivas didn't swoon at the sight of her rescuer. She sat up straight and squared her shoulders. Her breasts pushed forward, one of them almost out of the dislodged bra and torn blouse. Her clenched jaw and gritted teeth hardened her expression, but her voice was low and friendly.

"Always the hero. But that's your job. Right?"

"Not tonight. I'm off-duty. This one's on the house."

Gunshots sounded from the landing. A couple of shots from downstairs peppered the awkward silences and raised voices. Grant stood beside the open door from the front bedroom, his gun hanging loosely by his side. There was no need for the added threat it implied. He focused on Dominguez.

"Don't you find it off-putting?"

He nodded to the landing door.

"All that noise while you're playing Romeo and Juliet?"

Dominguez ignored the gun in Grant's hand. He spoke in a calm voice.

"You proceed from a false assumption again. This has nothing to do with betrayed romance but everything to do with betrayal."

Grant took another step into the room. "She supplied the info you needed. You're the one doing the betraying."

Dominguez shook his head. "She also supplied you. You weren't part of the deal."

Grant kept his gun hand loose. Ready for action.

"Now it's you proceeding from a false assumption. I just called round for a hot drink and a chat. Had nothing to do with her."

This time Dominguez smiled as he shook his head. "Do not treat me like a fool. Even you do not believe that."

He nodded towards Rivas.

"She certainly doesn't."

Rivas's shoulders sagged. Her eyes were dull and listless, the result of too many blows to the head tonight. She didn't look like she was completely focused. The drug baron from south of the border turned back to Grant. His tone hardened.

"You did not come here to arrest the Ukrainians. And you did not come here to upset me. You came here for some tender words in the middle of the night, and those tender words were from her."

He took a step towards Grant.

"Therefore, you are here because of her. And she is the reason you have caused me so much trouble."

"Aren't you forgetting the robbers and the Ukrainians?"

"The robbers we could have dealt with. The Ukrainians were always here. It is you who have been the fly in my ointment."

Grant caught movement in the corner of his eye. Rivas jerking her head toward the back of the room. Her shouted warning was loud and piercing—"Jim, watch out!"—but it was too late. The South American who'd brought her to the bedroom came out from behind the connecting door and slammed it against Grant's gun hand.

HOPE WAS PEERING OUT from the bathroom door when he heard the shout. He recognized the voice and knew the name. He hadn't developed a plan on how to find his tutor apart from keeping away from the gunmen and working his way to the garage. Most of the fighting was on the ground floor, forcing Hope to enter from the only place he knew was safe: upstairs. Apart from that, he was all at sea. Out of his depth. Youthful exuberance had taken over in the same way the young copper Grant had told him about had waltzed into the Chinese takeaway yelling cease and desist. This was more serious than a bunch of drunks fighting in the street.

Hearing Grant's name was a stroke of luck.

The gunmen backing up the stairs was not.

Gunshots blasted wood and plaster from the staircase. Two South Americans returned fire while edging up the stairs. Hope had a narrow window of opportunity before the battle spilled across the first floor landing. With a final glance at the warring parties, he dashed across the landing to the master bedroom.

Grant held onto the gun, but his wrist went numb and pain shot up his arm. The door slammed into him again, and he went down. The South American dropped both knees onto Grant's chest and knocked all the wind out of his lungs. Dominguez came over and stood on Grant's wrist. The pressure forced his fingers to open, releasing the gun. Dominguez bent to pick it up, then stood up straight. He let out a deep sigh as if he felt sad at how this was turning out.

"You should not have come here. Now you will never leave."

Rivas looked spent on the edge of the bed.

The South American forced his knees into Grant's chest.

Grant relaxed, taking in a couple of easy breaths, then letting them out slowly. His legs were bent slightly at the knees. His arms were pinned but loose. He needed to be ready when the opportunity arose.

Dominguez pulled up a chair from the dressing table and sat next to Grant.

"I have the greatest respect for the police force. The British police are the best in the world, despite those funny helmets. But I would have done your job for you"—he smiled, the oily charm returning—"and shut this operation down."

Grant looked into Dominguez's eyes. "You came all this way, in two helicopters, to close the Ukrainians down?"

"I did."

"That's very generous of you. I'll have to mention that in your defence."

"That won't be necessary. I shall be leaving soon."

"Having done my job for me."

"Just so."

"But taking the final shipment with you."

"It would be a shame to waste it."

Grant shifted his position beneath the man pinning him down. Dominguez nodded and the man lifted his weight, settling into a crouch beside the Yorkshire cop. Grant flexed his neck and filled his lungs.

"What were they doing? Exporting to America?"

Dominguez frowned. "They were exporting everywhere."

"That's why they were blackmailing the councillor? For exports?"

"I believe so. Yes."

"And they were cutting into your trade. All the way from Yorkshire."

"All the way from Europe. You're part of the EU now."

Grant raised his shoulders and rested back on his elbows. "You know, I get my car washed down the road from me—one of those handwash places. Six fellas spray it and mop it and power wash all the shit off. Next to the main road. Right here in Yorkshire. There's not a one of 'em's local. They're all Russians or Lithuanians or Poles or something. Came all the way here to clean my car. Just like you."

"I didn't come here to clean your car."

"You didn't come here to clean our drug problem either."

"But it is a happy side effect, no?"

"Not happy for everyone."

"Nothing ever is."

Grant tilted his head as if trying to remember something. He closed his eyes and let out a sigh.

When he opened them again, they focused on Dominguez. "I just had a thought. Before I came here tonight. My last job before going off-duty. We searched a house on Ravenscliffe. That's an estate over where I work. Well, we searched this house and found three bags of what you've got downstairs hidden under the bath. This kid, Lee Adkins, he also likes slapping women around. This kid supplies the estate. Sells it in little dealer baggies and makes a lot of money. Not as much as you. He can't afford two helicopters and a small army. But he gets by."

Grant's eyes hardened.

"Least he did before I shut him down. Like you've shut the Ukrainians down."

Dominguez leaned forward on the chair. "Is there a point to this?"

Grant nodded but didn't soften his gaze. "Point is, kids like Adkins are weeds. You pull one up and three grow in its place. So I'm guessing that now you've pulled this weed up we'll be getting three times as many bags of shit. Only they'll have a South American postmark."

He kept a track on the gun dangling from Dominguez's hand out of the corner of his eye and swivelled slightly on his back. His knees tensed, ready to move fast. He kept talking to keep Dominguez occupied.

"So how do you figure that's doing my job for me?"

Dominguez smiled. "You make a persuasive argument, but you can't avoid the natural law."

He let out a sigh and waved the gun for emphasis. "Nature abhores a vacuum. If you remove this supply, then another will always take its place. It just happens to be the Dominguez cartel filling the void."

The gun hand went limp again.

"You are the law. But it is the law of supply and demand that rules here. If there were no consumers, there would be no product to sell."

Grant edged one foot towards the nearest chair leg.

"That's a whole other argument. Might work with toothpaste. We all need to clean our teeth because we've all got teeth. You need to create drug addicts before you've got anybody to sell drugs to."

He flexed his knee and prepared to kick out.

Dominguez shook his head.

"You've got me there."

More gunshots sprayed the staircase and hallway. A ricochet punched through the plasterboard wall. Then the landing door burst open and Jamie Hope charged in as blue lights began flashing down at the truck stop.

06:30 HOURS

THE GUN CAME UP as soon as Dominguez saw the door burst open. Grant kicked out with his lead foot and snapped the chair leg off. The chair lurched to one side and Dominguez flayed his arms for balance. Grant shoved his shoulders backwards and caught the South American behind him under the shins. Crouching on his haunches wasn't a stable position. He tried to lunge forward, but his weight was going the wrong way. He tumbled onto his back.

Hope slammed the door shut as he stepped into the room. Dominguez regained his balance and stood up, kicking the chair out of his way. The South American rolled onto his side and began to get up. Grant was caught between the two of them. He could only defend against one. The sensible choice was to concentrate on the most dangerous: the man with the gun.

Dominguez swung his gun hand towards the intruder. He was sideways to the window. The blue flashing lights stood out against the darkness. He couldn't help the reflex to glance out of the window. That gave Grant a split second's extra time. He jabbed his right leg out straight and caught Dominguez just below the knee.

The leg hyperextended but didn't break. Dominguez went down hard, grabbing his knee with one hand while he tried to aim at Hope with the other. The gun went off, but the shot was high and wide. Grant couldn't get up quick enough to stop the second shot, but it was Rivas who saved the day.

She pushed off from the edge of the bed and lunged across the room, diving in front of the gun and grappling for the ugly black weapon in Dominguez's hand. The gun went off again. Grant was stunned to silence. He watched helplessly as Rivas body-checked Dominguez and landed on top of him. The gun skittered across the floor. Rivas lay still. Her eyes were wide and unblinking.

The South American managed to get up into a crouch and was turning toward Grant. He didn't even notice. He couldn't take his eyes off the waitress he'd been coming here to see for the last six months. The South American put a hand on the floor and pushed upwards. Jamie Hope took two steps and brought his knee up into the big fella's stomach. The cartel member doubled over and banged his face into the ground. Hope knee-dropped onto his spine and twisted one wrist behind his back. He shackled him to the wall radiator with the handcuffs he should have left at Ecclesfield Station, then stamped on Dominguez's knee for good measure. He turned to help Grant up.

Grant was already moving forward to turn Rivas over. Her face was pale apart from the blood and bruising down one side of her cheek. He cradled her in his arms, then she blinked and coughed and began patting herself down. There was no blood. There was no pain. There was just a scorched hole in the leather coat Grant had given her down by the wheelie bins.

She barked a harsh laugh and let out a sigh of relief.

Grant nodded but couldn't speak.

Hope stood up and looked out of the window at the blue lights. "Backup's here."

Grant ignored him. He puffed his cheeks out and let out a slow breath. The entire thing had only taken a couple of minutes, but it was long enough for the gun battle to have reached the first floor landing. He held Rivas in his arms a few seconds longer, then picked up the gun and helped her to her feet.

"Dumbwaiter."

She stared into his eyes. "Smile when you call me that."

He jerked a thumb at the adjoining room. "No. The dumbwaiter. Down to the garage. Time to go."

He ignored the South American handcuffed to the radiator and stepped over Dominguez rolling on the ground clutching his knee. Those things could be addressed once he'd hooked up with the ARVs who were deploying around the diner. Police tactics weren't gung ho like the marines storming a beachhead. They relied on safety and intelligence gathering. The intelligence gathering would be from units on the ground; the units on the ground were PCs Hope and Grant. He needed to tell the ARVs that the diner wasn't the threat anymore. The threat was the drug lab and warring cartels up at the house.

Grant picked up his gun and led Rivas into the front bedroom. Hope brought up the rear. None of them noticed Dominguez dragging himself to the landing door, his knee less painful than the thought of losing the shipment in the underground garage.

THE FIRST FLOOR LANDING was a war zone. The banister spindles were full of holes or blasted into ragged gaps like missing teeth. The three remaining South American gunmen were fighting a rear-guard action as they fell back against the back wall. They fired from a position of strength, holding the high ground and a wide selection of doorways for cover. Two of the Ukrainians worked their way up the stairs but couldn't storm the landing. They took potshots at the defenders but were never going to breach the first floor. The third covered their backs from the kitchen hallway.

The defenders saw the door of the master bedroom open and knew who it was before Dominguez poked his head through the gap. He was low to the ground to avoid stray bullets. From their angle on the stairs, the Ukrainians could only spray the upper walls and ceiling.

Dominguez barked instructions above the noise. "The basement. Three going down the service shaft."

The nearest gunman nodded at the stairs and shouted the obvious. "We're stuck."

Dominguez waved a hand to negate the attackers on the stairs. "Not through them. Around. Outside."

Then he jerked a thumb at the bedroom window.

"The police are at the diner. We need to get to the choppers."

The gunman glanced at his boss.

"Only one helicopter. The trucks took out the lower field."

Dominguez looked at the gleaming handcuffs shackling his companion to the radiator and thought about the other cop who'd come into the bedroom. Two flies in the ointment. He spat an angry curse in his own language. He forced himself up into a crouch, the strained tendons in his knee sending bursts of pain up his leg.

"Covering fire, then out. Fall back to the chopper."

The gunmen loosed two shots at the stairs. "What about the shipment?"

Dominguez shrugged off his pain and disappointment. "Forget the shipment. It was only icing on the cake. This operation is finished. The police will have it soon."

The gunman nodded. Dominguez glanced at the handcuffed South American, then drew his own gun from his belt. No witnesses. He shot the man in the head, then closed the door. His men followed their orders and gave covering fire as they moved towards the rear bedroom over the conservatory.

THE TRIP DOWN THE dumbwaiter shaft was faster than the climb up. Grant sent Hope down first, using the rope and pulley to slide down, then helped Rivas into the shaft. He instructed her on how to climb down, then watched her disappear into the darkness. The gunshots behind him were less frequent. The battle was waning. When he saw light spill into the shaft from the garage hatch, he swung his legs into the shaft and waited for Rivas to reach the bottom.

The rope creaked under his weight. He was taller and broader and heavier than the other two. He hoped the ancient twine would hold him. This was the final leg. A short trip down to the garage. Torch the fuel drums. Then open the door and reverse the Mercedes out into the snow. That was the plan.

THE TWO UKRAINIANS ON the stairs heard the shouted instructions and fell back from the weight of covering fire. They weren't in a strong position. All they could do was fire at the ceiling or blast out more of the banister rail. They couldn't see their targets from the stairs. That didn't matter. What mattered was what the lead South American had shouted across the landing.

"The basement. Three going down the service shaft."

That changed the gunmen's priorities. This was no longer about avenging their fallen comrades but about salvaging the shipment they had slaved over for the past two weeks.

One of them shouted down to the man covering their flanks. In their own language. *Secure the garage. Protect the shipment. Kill everyone.*

06:35 HOURS

Grant clambered out of the dumbwaiter hatch and stretched his legs. His back ached and his neck was stiff. There was a bruise on his forehead where he'd banged it during the slide down the shaft. Jamie Hope looked dishevelled and tired, the first time Grant had seen his probationer looking anything but neat and tidy. Wendy Rivas was the biggest transformation. Her crisp white waitress uniform was dirty and torn under the open jacket. Her face was caked in dried blood down one side and smudged with soot everywhere else. She looked like she'd climbed down a chimney.

That wasn't what worried Grant; it was the silence from upstairs. The gunfire had stopped. Either one side had killed the other or they'd reached a stalemate. He doubted if the warring gangs had joined forces and didn't think a standoff would provoke a ceasefire. It was also unlikely both sides had run out of ammunition at the same time. That left two choices. One gang was either dead or driven off. Whichever it was meant the other was free to regroup. Regrouping meant they could change priorities.

The priority now would be the shipment.

Grant scanned the garage for any changes since he'd left. It didn't take long. Nothing had changed. The Mercedes was still there. The stack of boxes was still there. And the fuel drums still leaked flammable liquid across the floor.

He focused on the drums.

The holes he'd punched with the screwdriver were halfway up the sides. Fuel oil lapped from the bottom hole of each drum, but it was just a trickle now. If Grant had been a glass-half-empty kind of fella, then he'd see that the drums had emptied to the lowest hole. What he saw was two oil drums half full of flammable liquid. Good. He also saw that the flood of fuel had spread across the concrete floor and run down the subbasement steps. Even better.

He took the Zippo lighter and the car keys out of his pocket. They were almost home free. There was just one last thing to do. He waved Hope towards the garage door controls. Hope nodded and began to cross the floor. Grant tossed the Mercedes keys to Rivas.

"Start the car."

She caught the keys in both hands and got in the driver's seat. The engine started first time. Hope reached out for the green button. Grant walked to the edge of the fuel stain and flicked the Zippo open. He let out a sigh of relief. They were going to make it. The wheel rasped and the flint sparked and the lighter burst into life. It was the last moment that everything was going according to plan. It was the closest they came to getting away clean.

Grant heard footsteps racing down the narrow staircase. He heard the garage door motor begin to hum. He tossed the lighter at the same time as he heard the gunshot.

Blue flame raced across the floor and turned orange as the fire took hold. The workbench caught light. The stacked boxes popped and crackled and burned a fierce yellow. The paint on the metal cabinet was stripped in seconds. The fluorescent light above the work area exploded in a shower of sparks.

Two Ukrainians spilled through the narrow doorway from the stairs. They split up, but the third man was slow in joining them. Shock lit their faces almost as bright as the orange flames. It froze them for an instant before the first man snapped out of it. His eyes flicked across the scene and his gun hand chose a target. He fired twice in quick succession.

The first bullet slammed Hope against the wall. The second dropped him to the floor. Lower back and top of his right leg. The leg was the worst. Blood gushed from the wound as the main artery ruptured. It ebbed and pulsed. Grant roared his anger and returned fire. Three shots. Two hits. Both in the same man. Upper body and shoulder. The gunman nearest the door spun to his right towards the blaze. His eyes flared with panic when he realized he was tumbling into the fire. He landed in a lake of liquid flames, and the fuel splashed over his clothes. He became a thrashing, screaming fireball.

The garage door crawled open. It seemed to take forever.

Twelve inches.

The snowdrift tumbled through the gap.

Eighteen inches.

The bottom of the ramp became visible.

Two feet.

Jamie Hope's blood soaked the snow.

Grant ignored the rising door and focused on defending his position. He was standing exposed in the middle of the floor. He couldn't move to his left because the fire had taken hold. The boxes were charring and falling apart. The bags of white powder were melting and catching fire. The heat was intense. If he moved to his right and used the car for cover he'd be drawing fire towards Rivas, who was lying across the front seats, out of sight.

There was only one thing for it. Make himself as small a target as possible and hit the enemy with everything he had. What he had was a handgun that had been fired several times and no spare magazine. He dropped to one knee and used single shots to keep the gunmen moving. The one that was left and the third man who came out of the narrow staircase.

Grant fired one shot at each man, then moved forward two feet.

He fired again and moved another two feet.

Both men ducked for cover. The only thing to hide behind was a pile of discarded packing cases and some tackle that had fallen off the wall. It didn't provide much protection. The shots ricocheting around their heads put them off their aim. They fired at Grant but missed wildly. It was one thing to shoot at stationary objects on a firing range and quite another to return fire when you could be dead at any moment. Very few men could remain calm under fire. Grant fired twice more, then the men broke cover and raced for the stairs. He fired one final shot into the doorframe, sending splintered wood into the staircase, then he slammed the door shut and dragged the tackle across to block it.

Jamie Hope was pale and motionless.

The pulsing blood spurts had dwindled to a trickle. Like the fuel oil trickling out of the oil drums, Hope was only half full. In reality he was as good as dead already. Grant didn't accept that. He shoved the gun into his waistband and dashed across the garage. The door was almost fully open. The snow had stopped, but it was still six inches deep across the ramp. Hope lay half in and half out of the door. The snow around him was bright red and spreading.

Grant dropped to a crouch and whipped his belt off. He quickly tied it around Hope's upper thigh and cinched it tight. The blood flow stopped, but Grant knew it was too late. His probationer had been shot twice, but only one shot had been needed. The lucky shot that blew out Hope's femoral artery. The lucky shot that came from the guns Grant had handed out to the Ukrainians for his diversion.

Hope's eyes flickered open. His voice was a whisper. "You were right."

Grant laid a finger on Hope's lips, but the probationer moved it aside. "About the warrant card thing."

Grant clenched his teeth and forced himself to stay calm.

Hope smiled. "They didn't cease and desist."

A sharp pain screwed up his face, and Grant laid a hand on his shoulder. He squeezed but said nothing. There was nothing to say. The pain eased, and Jamie Hope turned calm eyes on his tutor.

"I would have made a good copper."

This time Grant couldn't keep quiet. "You are a good copper."

Hope started to say something else but another spasm shook his body and he died in the snow. His faced became a mask. Grant reached down and gently closed his eyes. There was nothing left to say.

Rivas gunned the engine twice.

Grant looked over his shoulder.

Rivas jerked a finger towards the oil drums. The floor was a sea of flames licking at the bottom of the barrels. The ceiling cavity was filling with smoke. Flakes of white ash drifted in the thermals. The burned Ukrainian's gun began to jump as the shells in the magazine exploded. It was like the frying pan all over again, only more confined.

Rivas slipped the Mercedes into reverse and eased back towards the ramp. She shouted above the roar of the flames and the crackle of exploding ordnance.

"Jim."

She didn't need to say more. Time was short. They had to go. Grant looked into Hope's cold, blank face. Rivas raised her voice to a scream. "Leave him. We have to go. Now."

Grant snapped his head round and glared at Rivas. He nodded once, then slid his arms under Hope's back and legs. He jerked to his feet, carrying the body against his chest. Leave no man behind. An old army motto. It hadn't worked for him the last time in the desert, but he'd be damned if he was going to leave Hope to burn in this charnel house.

He shouted at Rivas. "Back door."

She reached behind the seat and opened the door. Grant leaned in and dropped Hope on the seat. The bullets stopped exploding. The wooden joists in the ceiling began to creak and groan. The metal cabinet ruptured in the heat and spilled cans of paint and thinners into the flames. They ignited into miniature flares.

Rivas gunned the engine.

Grant dived on top of Hope.

The Mercedes shot backwards through the garage door, building enough speed to carry it up the snow-covered ramp. The open car door was ripped off, but the rear-wheel drive and heavy tires bit into the snow with barely a sideways skid. The bumper clipped the edge of the retaining wall and deflected the car across the sloping driveway. The rear offside wheel arch careened off the opposite wall, then the Mercedes took off at the top of the ramp.

The oil drums finally reached flashover heat and exploded in a ball of flame that engulfed the garage and ripped through the charred ceiling into the ground floor. The fuel-soaked subbasement ignited, forcing expanded gasses and flames out of the air vents. Above the ground the three vent covers went off like firecrackers, the conical lids blasting into the pre-dawn sky. Inside the house, the interior walls were blown apart. The remaining windows shattered into glittering shrapnel.

The Mercedes landed in a skidding turn as blue flashing lights came up the service road from the diner. The ARVs had finally cleared the burned-out shell of the truck stop and were deploying towards the house. Grant ignored the cavalry that had come too late. As Rivas skidded to a stop, he sat up in the back seat and rested one hand on Jamie Hope's chest.

He felt drained and helpless. He didn't even notice the swirl of snow or the blinding spotlight as the second helicopter took off from the garden. None of that seemed important anymore. He patted Hope's chest, let out a deep sigh, and closed his eyes.

AFTERMATH

Grant crossed the car park behind Ecclesfield Police Station two weeks later wearing civilian clothes and his newfound favorite jacket, an orange windcheater with zip pockets and a furled hood in the collar. He paused at the No Smoking sign beside the dog kennels and felt anger build inside him all over again.

The battle at Woodlands Truck Stop and Diner made the news across the country and was even picked up in America due to the Dominguez cartel's alleged involvement. Alleged because there was no evidence to tie the South American gang to the Ukrainian drug factory behind the diner. Any bodies left behind in the house were burned beyond recognition. The only prisoners arrested at the scene feigned a lack of English and needed a Ukrainian translator, and even then they didn't say very much.

That only left the evidence of Jim Grant and Wendy Rivers, back to her Anglicized name, and that evidence was sketchy. Grant explained about Dominguez but couldn't give a first name or where he was from. He gave a written statement about the events of that Thursday night, concentrating on the heroism of probationer constable Jamie Hope. He left out the part about handing the guns back to the Ukrainians. There was more than enough for D&C to crucify Grant with without giving them anything else.

Wendy Rivers gave a statement too. Saying exactly what Grant had told her to say.

The Mercedes sank to its axles in the deep snow beyond the ramp. The house was fully ablaze, flames pouring out of the windows and doors and through a hole in the shingled roof where the chimney had collapsed into the attic. The blue flashing lights held off at the top of the service road, the ARVs deploying an extended perimeter as the firearms officers assessed the change of circumstances—mainly the house blowing up and the helicopter making good its escape.

And the smoking Mercedes that had just skidded to a halt.

Grant took a deep breath and opened his eyes. They were clear and focused, and his mind was back on the job at hand. The job at hand was identifying themselves to the armed police and then explaining what had happened with the least amount of collateral damage.

"Wendy. Listen to me."

Rivas turned the engine off, her hand shaking on the key. Her face was pale beneath the blood and dirt. Her eyes blinked until she shook herself free of the adrenalin rush that gripped her body. The engine ticked and cooled. Steam rose from the bodywork as heat from the blazing garage subsided. Grant leaned forward between the front seats.

"Best thing here is to keep it simple."

Rivas's shoulders sagged. The bravado and excitement fell away to reveal a frightened woman who had scouted for the Dominguez cartel and now had to face the music. Grant recognized that and began turning it around.

"Your name is Wendy Rivers."

That got her eyes working.

Grant spoke in measured tones, keeping his words simple.

"Tell it exactly as it happened. The robbery. The Ukrainians. The helicopters at the house. Everything that happened. What didn't happen was you working here to provide info for the cartel."

Her eyes filled with hope.

Grant nodded.

"You're the night waitress. That's all."

A half smile feathered her lips.

"And you're the policeman."

"Not tonight. I'm off-duty. We're both just innocent bystanders."

Her voice was filled with regret.

"Some more innocent than others."

Shadows moved across the blue flashing lights. The snow was intermittently dark and foreboding, then brilliant icy blue. Grant felt the night drawing to a close. Dawn was lightening the sky on the eastern horizon. His pulse wasn't much above normal. That was one of the benefits of remaining calm under pressure. He never got the adrenalin rush or the subsequent letdown when it subsided. He never dwelled on the mistakes he had made. Not for long, anyway.

"Everyone's guilty of something."

Rivers shifted in her seat and turned to look Grant in the eye. "Will I see you again?"

Grant looked towards the diner. "Well, there's nowhere left for midnight tea."

Her voice softened. "You know what I mean."

Grant kept any emotion out of his voice, aiming for straight and professional, but it wasn't easy. He'd always thought this might lead to something. The police officer and the waitress.

"There might be a trial. Maybe not. You'll be a witness. After that, I think you should go back home. Change your name. Start afresh. Stay away from anyone called Dominguez."

He raised a hand and stroked her cheek. "You can serve coffee and donuts to some real cops."

She covered his hand with hers. "You are a real cop."

"I'm a suspended cop. Probably suspended from the nearest tree after tonight."

Rivers leaned through the gap and kissed him gently on the lips. "Tonight. You were my hero."

That made Grant feel good. The body lying beside him on the back seat brought him back down to earth. "No. I'm his tutor. I'm responsible. Gonna have to face up to that."

The shadows angled across the car. Three men moved in unison. A gruff voice shouted orders. Grant nodded for Rivers to comply. Then he got out of the car with his hands open and his arms held out like a cross.

THE KENNELS WERE EMPTY. There was no smoke drifting from the illegal smoking area. Grant ignored the memory of his last encounter here and went in the back door to the police station. The corridors were empty. At this time in the afternoon, the late shift were all out on patrol. The only part of the police station that was fully staffed was the admin offices on the first floor. The pencil pushers and the typists and the senior management team. The top brass who had climbed the promotion ladder to the point where they weren't really coppers anymore.

Grant checked his tray in the report writing room. It was empty apart from his payslip. His workload had been distributed among the rest of the shift—crime reports, vehicle enquiries, outstanding warrants; the stuff that frontline police have to deal with. The fact that Grant's had been reallocated didn't bode well. The fact that he'd been called in from his suspension in civvies was even worse.

He put the payslip in his pocket and went back along the corridor. The shift inspector's office was on the first floor. A gatekeeper to the senior management team to whom he answered. Police inspectors were the tools of the bosses. The real power lay with the shift sergeants. Sergeant Ballhaus came out of his office as Grant walked past.

"You on your way up?"

Grant was glad to see a friendly face. "He wants to see me."

Ballhaus stood in the doorway, blocking the view into the office. "You want me to come with you?"

Grant tried to read his sergeant's expression.

"Do I need you to come with me?"

Ballhaus shrugged. "I don't think so."

There was movement in the office behind the sergeant. Ballhaus couldn't block it all out. The voice that came over his shoulder raised Grant's hackles.

"If it was up to me, you'd need a friend and a Federation rep and a good judge."

Nelson Carr stepped into the doorway. The D&C inspector was taller than the sergeant and looked over the top of Ballhaus's head.

The grin he flashed was harsh and humorless. Light glinted off his gold fillings. Grant tried to keep the anger off his face.

"Bulldog Drummond. Haven't lost your fillings yet, I see."

"And you haven't lost your cavalier attitude."

Grant stared into the D&C bulldog's eyes. "You remember that song—the one in Monty Python's *Life of Brian*?"

He began to whistle "Always Look on the Bright Side of Life." Ballhaus smiled. Carr bristled. Grant nodded at his sergeant and was about to walk away when Carr threw a final barb.

"Couldn't make it to the funeral, then?"

Grant froze with his back to the D&C inspector. They had buried Jamie Hope at Nab Wood Cemetery with full honors and a graveside ceremony. The entire shift had attended in full dress uniform. Words had been spoken. Tributes made. There had been silence and reflection and not a few tears. Grant had watched it all from the tree line overlooking the cemetery.

He considered responding to the taunt but didn't want to cheapen Hope's memory. Instead he squared his shoulders and headed for the stairs.

THE SHIFT INSPECTOR WAS sitting at his desk when Grant knocked and opened the door. Inspector Speedhoff had ginger hair and a ruddy complexion that was renowned for flaring up under pressure. He often went red in the face when shift briefings got out of hand. His face was pale and colorless when he gestured Grant towards the chair in front of his desk.

Speedhoff seemed calm and almost jovial, an unusual combination since Grant had always been considered a thorn in the inspector's side. Grant's straight-talking, down-and-dirty methods went against the grain of modern statistics-led policing. Kicking in doors and browbeating suspects weren't Speedhoff's MO.

Grant sat in the chair and waited.

Speedhoff finished signing some papers, slipped them into a buff folder, then put his pen away. The office was quiet. Somewhere in the distance a siren indicated that real police work was being done. Along the corridor, in the admin block, the gentle clickety-clack of typing mingled with the babble of female voices. Somebody laughed. A car sped past the police station with a squeal of tires.

Speedhoff's voice aimed for friendly. He almost achieved it. "You been downstairs?"

Grant wasn't going to make it easy for him. "Got to. It's the only way to get upstairs."

Speedhoff's face reddened. "Yes, quite. Did you speak to anyone?"

Grant wondered where this was going. "Bumped into Sergeant Ballhaus. Inspector Nelson had a few words. He's not a happy bunny."

Speedhoff saw his chance to get back on track. "He wouldn't be. He's just been in to see the divisional commander."

The inspector smiled. The redness faded. He could obviously see a way out of all his problems. Grant noticed that the buff folder was half turned towards him. His name was written across the top. Speedhoff rested his arms on the desk.

"I wanted to tell you personally. The Lee Adkins complaint has been dropped."

Grant raised his eyebrows. "How come?"

Speedhoff continued in a friendly tone. "The broken ribs were caused by the girl."

"Sharon Davis?"

"She kicked out at him during the assault and caught him one on the chest. She has also decided to give a statement and press charges against him."

Grant was calculating in his head. "What about the drug offences?"

Speedhoff shook his head. "Sorry. No. The breach of protocol, as evidenced by PC Hope, remains. The subsequent arrest and house search are negated. We can't take him to court for the supplying, I'm afraid."

The mention of Jamie Hope's name brought a cloud over Grant's head. He shifted in his seat and lowered his voice. "Yeah, well. His supply dried up at Snake Pass."

Speedhoff cleared his throat and drummed his fingers on the desk. "Yes. That's the other thing."

Grant interrupted him. "Hang on. Does that mean my suspension is lifted?"

Speedhoff nodded, but the gesture morphed into him shaking his head. "Yes and no. For assaulting Adkins, yes. But then there is this other thing."

Grant wasn't going to make this easy for him either.

"This other thing being Snake Pass?"

Speedhoff stopped drumming his fingers. He took a deep breath and proceeded to spout the party line.

"On the one hand, you have single-handedly identified and dismantled a major international drug manufacturing operation and uncovered a blackmail plot against a prominent local councillor."

Grant recognized the hand-me-down words from the senior management team.

"Not single-handed. Jamie Hope gave his life protecting the…"

He couldn't finish. He took a deep breath and shook his head.

Speedhoff appeared to feel Grant's pain. He paused for a moment to let the constable gather himself before continuing.

"That is the plus side. The downside is that it involved fourteen deaths, four vehicles being torched, and two buildings destroyed. There will be a full enquiry into the circumstances of those actions. And you will be the center of that investigation."

The inspector bowed his head. He brought both hands up to rub his temples. When he looked at Grant again, his face showed sympathy and understanding that Grant hadn't thought Speedhoff was capable of. The Team Two inspector smiled with a hint of sadness.

"Look. Let's cut to the chase. You did a great job, but the cost was high. There are questions that need answering. But the media have painted us into a corner. D&C can't come after you without tarnishing the conquering hero."

Grant was beginning to see where this was going. "So that's why Inspector Carr looks so pissed off."

"He will be leading the investigation, but his teeth have been pulled. As far as the chief constable's office is concerned, Snake Pass is a done deal. We just need to keep you out of the way while the dust settles."

Now Grant wasn't so sure. He waited for the hammer to drop.

Speedhoff opened Grant's folder and slid out the piece of paper he'd just signed.

"We're sending you on an out-of-force enquiry. Interview a prisoner being held cross-border. A quick interview to eliminate him from a burglary in our division. Freddy Sullivan."

Grant knew Freddy Sullivan, but this didn't make sense. "I thought he'd emigrated to—"

"America. Yes. They're holding him at Jamaica Plain in Boston."

Grant smiled. Sergeant Ballhaus had been right all the way back at Edgebank Close. If Grant fell in a pile of shit, he'd come up smelling of roses. Speedhoff leaned back in his chair.

"I hope your passport's up to date."

THE END

ACKNOWLEDGMENTS

It's morphing time again, when I go from solitary writing to multiple collaboration—when the book goes from my words on paper to the book you see before you. As always, that takes the efforts of many people, to all of whom I owe a debt of thanks. Rebecca Zins ironed out the flaws. Terri Bischoff saw the big picture. And my agent, Donna Bagdasarian, brought us all together. The last person in that chain is you, the reader. Without you, I wouldn't keep morphing into a writer. Thank you all.

The following excerpt is from

JAMAICA PLAIN

Book 1 in the Resurrection Man Series
by Colin Campbell.

The first thing Jim Grant did when he landed in Boston was buy a map. The second thing was get laid. The third was almost get himself killed interviewing a prisoner who was into something far bigger than what the detective came to interview him about.

Detective. That sounded good, but Grant knew it was only a temporary assignment while his inspector cleaned up the mess he'd left behind in Yorkshire. He was still just a plain old constable: PC 367 Grant. Maybe while he was visiting the US he should think of himself as a cop. Then again, maybe not. That would be going a bit too Hollywood.

First things first. If he were going to find his way around Boston, he'd need a map. Ignoring the other passengers collecting their wheeled cases from the luggage carousel, Grant hefted the battered leather holdall in one hand and went in search of the concession stands. That was his first mistake. Three thousand miles from home, and trouble still managed to find him straightaway.

Logan International was bigger than Manchester Airport, but the basics were the same. Wide open spaces, big windows looking out onto the runways, and dozens of preformed waiting-room chairs in rows of four with a low table in between, all connected so if one person sat down, all four seats bounced. Grant had lost count of how many cups of coffee he'd spilled because some heavyweight couldn't lower himself into his seat.

The place smelled of plastic and canned air.

There were fewer seats in the arrivals lounge than in departures. Fewer people wanted to sit down after spending a long flight cramped in a seat with no legroom and someone in front leaning back so that what little room you did have was crushed against your knees. At least that was Grant's experience of international travel. At six feet four he'd have troubling stretching out in first class. West Yorkshire Police hadn't paid for first class. Prisoner extradition might have warranted the expense. Getting your bad egg out of the way meant the cheapest seat available and forget the legroom.

Logan had one other thing in common with Manchester. Airports attracted criminals like flies around shit. For some reason, Grant was the embodiment of human flypaper. He wasn't looking, but his eyes couldn't help roving. It was a reflex action. Any room he entered, the first thing he'd do was scan the crowd, quickly followed by a check of the exits and any mirrors that could be used for extra viewing. He never sat anywhere he couldn't see behind him. He never stood anywhere he couldn't get out of fast if trouble started.

This wasn't trouble. It was two kids dipping pockets and doing it very well.

Distraction was the main technique for most crimes apart from blatant armed robbery. Thieves didn't want to get caught, so it was better if nobody saw what they were stealing. Burglars usually broke in at night. Thieves usually stole when nobody was looking. Only complete idiots or hardened criminals stuck a gun in your face and demanded your money. The victims would remember you for the rest of their lives. Some might even shoot you. If nobody saw you take their wallet, then who was going to be a witness in court? Nobody.

Movement and noise were the best distractions. An airport arrivals lounge had plenty of both. Everyone was in a rush. Suitcases were being wheeled around. Visitors were looking for their relatives. Airport transfer drivers were milling around with name cards written in thick black letters. People were buying coffee, magazines, and maps.

Grant was paying for the Boston street map at Hudson News when he spotted the teenage tag team. Their target was an attractive woman in a business suit he'd seen at the luggage carousels. Tidy figure. Tight trousers. Nice arse. He focused on that for a while, but his peripheral vision saw the hunters circling. Part of his brain wanted to chat with the businesswoman. Part of him wanted to arrest the pickpockets. The rest of him remembered his inspector giving a stern warning before setting off.

Keep out of trouble. Don't get involved. You're off-duty.

That wasn't strictly true. This was a holiday assignment, yes. Interview the prisoner. Eliminate him from the inquiry. Release him and come home. He'd been sent on it to keep him out of the way while Discipline and Complaints investigated the mess at Snake Pass. But he'd be on-duty during the interview, and technically you were on-duty while traveling to and from work for the purposes of injury-on-duty claims. Have an accident on the way to work and it was classed as an injury on-duty. So if he spotted a crime on his way to work…

Keep out of trouble. Don't get involved.

That part went against the grain. If there was one thing Jim Grant found hard to do, it was ignore a crime right in front of his face. Bad guys did bad things. It was up to the good guys to stop them. Grant was one of the good guys. Always had been. Keeping out of trouble should be easy with a pair of teenagers. Maybe thirteen or fourteen. It just required a bit of tact.

He paid for the map and watched.

THE TEENAGE BOY WAS very good. The girl was even better. What they had going for them was how innocent they both looked. Butter wouldn't melt in their mouths, you'd think. Grant watched them hanging around outside the magazine stand. They appeared to be waiting for their parents—only they weren't watching for someone joining them, they were scouring the shoppers for easy marks.

The businesswoman wheeled her suitcase into the shop, an expensive shoulder bag hanging open around her back. The boy nodded. The girl split off and held position ten feet away. The dance began.

The woman bought a pack of breath mints and an orange juice. The boy stayed a few feet behind her. The girl kept station ten feet away. When the woman left the shop, the boy followed. The girl never let the distance alter—ten feet—until the boy nodded again. The girl moved in front and bumped into the woman. The boy's hand was so fast Grant hardly saw it. In and out of the bag in a flash. He broke left and the girl apologized, going right. A quick half-circle and they crossed paths. A dull brown shape was switched, and now it was the girl, all cute and innocent, with the stolen goods. The woman didn't even know she'd been targeted.

Don't get involved.

Not an option. Grant moved quick, before the boy and girl separated too far. Without being obvious, he grabbed the boy's arm and guided him towards the girl. He identified himself as police and told the girl to follow them. She did. Fear shone in her eyes. Caught in the act. It was the look every kid he'd ever arrested had the first time. He didn't squeeze. There was no need. The threesome gathered by a water fountain against the wall.

"Okay, kids. I haven't got time for this. Hand it over."

The girl's eyes darted at the boy and then over his shoulder. The boy had no resistance. The girl gave Grant the wallet. He kept half an eye on the teenagers and the other half on the businesswoman. She had stopped to take a drink of orange juice and drop the mints in her bag. Grant towered over the teenagers.

"Now beat it. You won't be so lucky next time."

Without waiting for an answer, he set off across the concourse. The woman was on her second swig of juice when he held the wallet out. "I think you dropped this."

Her first reaction was to look him in the eyes. A hard, straight look that sized him up in an instant. Big guy in worn jeans and a faded orange windcheater. Then she reverted to victim mode. She swung the shoulder bag round front and rummaged inside. Grant handed the wallet over. Gratitude feathered a smile across her lips. A twinkle in her eyes. "What sharp little eyes you've got."

"Not so little."

"No, you aren't, are you?"

This was interesting. Grant was about to explore the possibilities when he saw the teenagers over the woman's shoulder. The fear in the girl's eyes had multiplied tenfold. The angry man herding them away didn't look like their father.

Keep out of trouble.

That didn't look like an option now either. The man was big in a lumpy fat man sort of way. There was bulk and muscle, but he was out of shape. That didn't matter when it came to intimidating kids. The kids looked plenty intimidated. The girl looked terrified.

"Excuse me."

Grant dodged around the woman and set off after Fagin. The man looked angry they'd missed picking the latest pocket or two. The grip he exerted on the boy was harder than Grant's had been. He didn't need to grip the girl. She'd go wherever the boy went. Loyalty. An admirable quality. Grant was glad he'd let them go. He wasn't glad he'd steered them into this spot of bother.

Fagin took the pair round the corner into an alcove between the left luggage office and the restrooms. As soon as he was out of sight, he slapped the boy round the back of the head. Bad move.

Grant heard the slap before he came around the corner. Heard the boy's muted cry and the girl's whimper. He switched the holdall into his right hand, freeing up his stronger left. He was a lefty. Conflict was unavoidable, and his instincts took over. Calmness settled over him. It was his combat preparation, a technique that had served him well in the army and worked just fine as a frontline cop. Most people tensed up in the line of fire. Grant did the opposite. He relaxed. His muscles became loose. His mind smoothed out any wrinkles. Nothing obstructed the flow of action. Nothing deflected his point of focus.

His point of focus now was a fat man picking on a couple of kids.

Grant came around the corner like a force of nature. He swung the holdall and let go. It sailed out and upwards, catching Fagin by surprise. Fagin instinctively turned and caught it in both arms. That left no hands free and Grant with two. He only needed one. The strong left hand grabbed Fagin by the shoulder and pushed him backwards. The right hand stayed loose just in case. Momentum and the heavy bag propelled Fagin towards the restrooms. Grant guided him through the door into the gents'.

The door swung shut behind them.

"What the fuck?"

Fagin found his tongue and rediscovered some of his bravado. He held the holdall across his chest like a shield, flexing his shoulders and giving his head a little nudge forwards like a boxer ducking and diving. He wasn't any boxer. Tension etched itself on his face. Surprise factor had won the first round.

"Fuck you think you're doin'?"

Grant surged forward and shoved the holdall hard. The bag was heavy. The left hand was heavier. Height and weight and muscle were all in Grant's favor. The blow transferred through the bag and thumped Fagin in the chest like a sledgehammer. He stumbled backwards and came up against the washbasins. Grant stood in front of him and slightly off-center to avoid being kicked in the gonads.

"I know just what I'm doing."

He stepped to the side and raised one leg slightly. He stamped on the outside edge of Fagin's left leg below the knee, and the overweight bully collapsed like a broken twig.

"And that's my bag you've got there."

He snatched the holdall left-handed and swung it in a short underarm arc. The weight of it multiplied on the back swing. It grew even more on the follow-through. Grant leaned into the swing, staying relaxed but with his feet apart for a solid base, and brought the bag forward hard and fast. It caught Fagin under the chin and snapped his head back against the built-in marble-topped washbasins.

He flopped like a boned fish. No spine. All wet.

Three men using the basins down the row quickly collected their bags and dashed out of the restroom. The hot-air hand dryer one of them had been using kept working for a few seconds. An automatic faucet dribbled cold water. The door flip-flapped shut like the swing doors of a Western saloon. The water stopped. The hand dryer switched itself off. Hot metal ticked as it cooled.

Grant nudged Fagin awake with his foot, then dragged him into a sitting position by the collar. He instinctively reached for the handcuffs on his hip before realizing he was plainclothes. No protective equipment. No handcuffs. Off-duty.

He stood up and to one side. The most dangerous beast is a cornered animal. A fighting arc didn't just mean a swinging fist. A well-aimed kick could bring down even the strongest man. Grant kept out of kicking range even though Fagin didn't look like he had a good kick left in him. He switched the bag to his right hand, freeing up his left.

"That's theft. Now why do you want to take stuff that don't belong to you?"

"I don't take stuff that's not mine."

Grant dropped the holdall onto Fagin's outstretched legs and knelt down on it fast and heavy, pinning the fat man and bringing Grant's face right into Fagin's personal space. Grant's strong left hand came up, and Fagin flinched. Grant didn't hit him. He grabbed his nose between thumb and forefinger and twisted. Blood and snot oozed like a squeezed tube of toothpaste.

"No, you don't, do you? You get kids to take it for you."

Fagin moaned in pain. Grant twisted harder.

"They your kids?"

"No."

The word came out all mashed but just about intelligible.

"Whose?"

Fagin tried to speak and flapped a hand towards his nose. Grant let go.

"City orphanage."

"Wrong. They're my kids now. See what happens if you touch them again."

He didn't finish. Instead he stood up and washed his hands. The hand dryer was still hot. He dried his hands. There wasn't even a hint of post-action adrenaline shakes—another benefit of Grant's relaxation technique. He picked the bag up and went to the door.

"You're lucky I'm on vacation. That's what you call a holiday over here, isn't it?"

He pushed the swing door and reentered the world of noise and movement. *Keep out of trouble. Don't get involved.* One out of two wasn't so bad. He wasn't surprised that the kids had gone. What did surprise him was who had stayed.

"You're not that small at all, are you?"

The businesswoman smirked. Grant smiled. He looked down at her from a great height and flexed the muscles of his neck. Bones cracked like firecrackers. He lowered his voice. "You know what I could do with right now?"

"I think I do. Welcome to Boston."

ABOUT THE AUTHOR

Ex-Army, retired cop, and former scenes-of-crime officer Colin Campbell is also the author of British crime novels *Blue Knight, White Cross* and *Northern eX*. His Jim Grant thrillers bring a rogue Yorkshire cop to America, where culture clash and violence ensue. For more information, visit www.campbellfiction.com.